We Are Taking Only What We Need

This Large Print Book carries the
Seal of Approval of N.A.V.H.

WE ARE TAKING ONLY WHAT WE NEED

STORIES

STEPHANIE POWELL WATTS

THORNDIKE PRESS
A part of Gale, a Cengage Company

Farmington Hills, Mich • San Francisco • New York • Waterville, Maine
Meriden, Conn • Mason, Ohio • Chicago

LIBRARY OF CONGRESS CIP DATA ON FILE.
CATALOGUING IN PUBLICATION FOR THIS BOOK
IS AVAILABLE FROM THE LIBRARY OF CONGRESS

ISBN-13: 978-1-4328-5573-4 (hardcover)

Published in 2018 by arrangement with Ecco, an imprint of
HarperCollins Publishers

Printed in Mexico
1 2 3 4 5 6 7 22 21 20 19 18

To Bob and Auden, the loves of my life

CONTENTS

CONTENTS

INTRODUCTION

When I was a kid we moved around a lot. We didn't always move out of town and never out of the state of North Carolina, and often our move was just a few streets or neighborhoods over from where we started. I can't remember the first time we moved when I knew for sure it would only be temporary, that there would always be another pack-up, another move — a few months, maybe a year at the most down the line.

I do, however, remember our first move. After my parents' divorce, my mother, two of my four brothers, and I left our dirt road for a house in the next small town. The house was old though not charmingly so, definitely in *before* condition, and surrounded by many other tiny, rundown houses. It wasn't all bad, though. Even now, more than thirty years later, I think of the to-the-ceiling white kitchen cabinets and the phone niche in the hallway with some fondness. For the few months we lived there, we stumbled over boxes, trash bags of clothes, toys, and miscellaneous junk hastily piled anywhere there was space. We did not stay at this house long enough to fully unpack.

I remember being so excited. I know this is hard to believe, but moving was a great adventure. Life was different then. The people we knew were skinny and poor and drove around in dogs of cars and counted out money from their piggy banks at the end of the month for gas. We did not travel. We knew nothing of the world. We marveled at the middle-aged white people we knew from school or work that had been to Paris, France, and London, England, and could prove it with slides. We didn't have disposable income — that wasn't even a phrase we knew yet — and everyone we knew lived frugally by necessity. I remember my mother and a friend talking about another friend who was having such hard times she had to use a credit card at the grocery store! I've thought of their conversation many times when I'm paying for bananas and a carton of milk with my Visa.

My mother was convinced and convincing, and every time she felt the need, she sold us on the idea that this next move would change our lives. She believed in the power of place as the springboard for our reinvention. Anything was possible this time. The slate of our existence would be wiped clean and we would get to rethink and redo everything. I caught her enthusiasm. I loved the anticipation of the move, the process of going through our possessions and deciding what was worthy enough to make the trip to a new life. Those too baggy shorts, toss; the once-loved blouse with the impossible stain, out. We had to travel light. We had room only for the good. My mother's motto could have been, "Change your address and change your life. This time we are going to get everything just right."

I have since learned that a good number of poor women with their children move with regularity. But at the time, when I was young, I knew of only one other kid who moved around like I did. She had come from a big city and told me in one of our true confession sessions that her mother could not stay put. The last move my friend made in childhood had been to North Carolina when her mother left her in the care of her grandmother and had not returned. I learned then the power of a secret to seal a relationship. Tell me a secret and I give you my trust. I had imagined all that time that I was the only one coming to school red-eyed and exhausted after spending most of the night unpacking boxes. But I have learned as a grown person that there is no malady, or pathology in this wide world that someone else isn't suffering right along with you. Mothers all over the country and from every walk of life, like my mom, scrape together every penny they have, set their sights on a new place, and start over. I get it. The urge for change, any life-altering change, is strong. The desperate need for control of anything at all is even stronger. Moving is kinetic and purposeful at just a time when the world seems most out of control. The mind needs diversion from constant trouble and grows weary from weariness, tired from constant fatigue. The mind can focus only so long on lack or pain or loneliness, and needs a persistent and consuming outlet that feels necessary. Pack everything you own, stuff the kids in the car. Find the right house or apartment and find the right life.

I have been thinking a lot about moving since my family bought a new house (new to me) in Allentown, Pennsylvania. My young child did not want the change. *I love our home, mama, I don't want to leave.* The old feeling of excitement and dread and the thrill of *maybe this time* that I thought I'd buried too deep to access welled up, but now I was the pleading mama. "You will love it, honey. We will be near a park. Your room will be so beautiful. Everything will be just like you want it." It wasn't just talk. I was willing happiness into being, insisting on it. I would not tell my sweet son that being on the move made me feel like an outsider, but like a seeker too. I still worry that in the rest and the nesting that the seeker discovers that no room can ever truly fit, no apartment, no house has space enough for the seeker's great and consuming needs.

I have not lived with my mother for more than a generation now. It has been a long time since I've felt her enthusiasm sweeping me all along to the next house and the next bright future. Somehow even after all this time, I feel the tickle of desire every two or three years to pack the car, leave the broken and unloved detritus behind, travel two streets or two towns over, and start again. Everybody in the car together.

The stories in my collection are about young African American women trying to find their homes in the world. The stories are set in North Carolina in the new south, postsegregation, post–Jim Crow, post-lawful separation of races, but those ghosts endure. My characters are usually poor, but not content to be so. They are usually watchers, but at crucial moments are compelled to act. They are girls determined to be proud women. The world has a place for them and they will find it. And some of them will find that place that can finally feel like home.

FAMILY MUSEUM OF THE ANCIENT POSTCARDS

In April 1976 my uncle Silas on my daddy's side got out of jail early after two years and five months of time served for arson. We welcomed him with dinners and back slaps, ignored the pink guilty splotches on his face, places on his skin that would never fully heal, regarded him with a child's wonder, his disappearing act a magic trick, now you don't, but now you do see him.

July '76 was the bicentennial for white people, and though we agreed with our black Muslim cousin and black nationalist neighbor, "whose 200 years of freedom?" we all marveled at the fireworks in town, bigger and better than usual, some of us with our arms crossed over our chests in protest, but all of us with faces tilted to the clear summer sky.

But most remarkably, late in that year, forty-one-year-old Ginny Harshaw, my mother's aunt's child, my cousin, though I called her Aunt Ginny, found a husband. We'd given up on her long, long ago. But just when she had ceased to be a variable in the world of change, Aunt Ginny shocked us with Gerald, five foot, maybe a little more, with a big round belly taut as a starving child's. Though Aunt Ginny was an imposing woman, tall and big boned, a woman's beautiful, "her cheekbones," the women said, her "long fingers like a pianist," they said, though no man ever noticed, apparently, except for Gerald.

Our family talked. My mother, her sisters and brothers, wives of brothers, everyone had something to say about Aunt Ginny and Gerald. But none of our mocking importance or our jokes made Aunt Ginny twist in shame or doubt the certainty of her mind. Nothing stopped her from rushing like a teenager out her mama's door when Gerald's Gran Torino rattled up the drive. "He is not afraid," she said, and neither was she as she launched herself into the world, sprung and released like a sharp stone from a slingshot. After all those years of living with her mother and her dead father, gone now for twenty-five of those years, she finally flew the coop. On the way out the door, her hard suitcase on the porch already (she would return for her personal things

16

soon, she said), pillowcases of summer clothes packed in the trunk of Gerald's car, she bent to her mother's chair in the front room, her hair dyed black as a China-woman's, tickled Aunt Ginny's lips, "Bye Mama," she said. Once on the porch, she threw a kiss to her father. "Thank you, merciful God," she said aloud. At that same moment, she thought she'd never again have to hear her father's dead steps in the attic or behind her, no more heavy breath, sour from old cigarettes, lingering in the dark places of the creaky house he put together with his own hands. *Enough, Enough,* she thought, not sure if what she felt wasn't ecstasy. Poor Aunt Ginny. She didn't know (how could she?) how dangerous and fool-ish it is to count on anything for the rest of your life.

We didn't hear much from Aunt Ginny in those early months, though we saw her every week on Sunday at my grandmother's. She stayed close to Gerald, served him food like the other wives, patted his hand, looked at him with what we thought was longing when he stood up too early to take her back to their home. We tried to get him to talk and included him the best we knew how. His people weren't neighbors or friends of ours; they were poor blacks, what we called Boomer rats, who lived many in dark houses out on tangled dirt roads on the fringes of the county. Our own dirt roads and tiny houses where we lived were exempt from judgment. We thought we could make nice talk, let him know he was free to sit among us. We told him how Ginny cooked the best turkey, juicy, we said. Years ago, we said, Ginny's hair was a marvel, black and shiny as a satin sheet, long enough for her to sit on. One time, a white man tried to buy it right off her head in Charlotte. Ginny would run her hand through her now-short curls embarrassed to have all that past called up. And though nobody told it, Aunt Ginny knew we were all thanking Gerald for making her (the one we'd all called *the lost cause*) as normal as any of the other women. Gerald nodded, squinted his eyes in concentration. "Is that right?" was the most he'd say.

A couple of times Aunt Ginny came to Sunday dinner alone, dumb and still as a cow, waiting for the best moment to make her excuses and leave. But soon, though no one is sure exactly when, Aunt Ginny stopped coming at all. "Too far," she said. "Busy, you know how it is," she said, deepening her voice, hinting at sexual delights

18

she hoped the long-married women remembered and coveted. But we knew Gerald was to blame. He had been the only person to change Ginny, the only one to make her want to snap her inertia and escape, shedding the kidnapper's ropes and leaving them in a snaky heap behind her. Whatever roots he worked, prayers or curses he hurled on the air, we knew without fighting it that it was powerful magic. Our best hope was that Aunt Ginny was too happy not to play along with Gerald. We were, of course, disappointed.

Almost eight months after her departure, Aunt Ginny came back to us, with her lips grim and set in a freeze that even death couldn't remove. Aunt Ginny rode shotgun beside her mother in the passenger seat of the Buick, her clothes in pillowcases in the back seat, the hard case luggage, a high school graduation present, forgotten in the rush.

"My nerves can't take all this," Aunt Ginny's mother said as she parked in the drive, theatrically lumbering to her chair in the front room. "You ought not put me through it." Her clothes out of the car, Aunt Ginny rested in her room, tried not to look at the lumpy pillowcases leaking her panties and hastily stuffed polyester from their open tops. She kicked the bag off the edge of the bed, and the rags exploded like confetti on the floor. "I'm back, bastard," she whispered, sure her father had heard.

We wouldn't say it to her. We are not cruel, but we knew all along Aunt Ginny would return. Late marriages can't take; we nodded in agreement. The old are tired, sapless and try it, be our guest, but you can't make it without hope, the antidote to despair, that the old have irretrievably lost. Though we wanted different for her, we knew Aunt Ginny's story would take one of just a few predictable shapes. The way they told it, Gerald beat Aunt Ginny for being tall, for glancing at him without tenderness as he drifted to sleep, for trying to prove that he could be loved. Aunt Ginny would not say, but something brought her home in a hurry. We thought we understood.

Aunt Ginny tried; you have to give her that. We saw her trying, felt her stretching for something good. We knew that what she wanted was that glad day when the life with Gerald that she knew was just around the corner finally materialized, poof, in a cloud of sorcerer's smoke. "You'll learn fooling with low class niggers," Aunt Ginny's mother said, the smug joy in her heart obvious on her face, a cruel, cutting brightness like a sunny winter sky. Now, Aunt Ginny would have no reason to ever again refute what her mother told her.

I suppose Aunt Ginny's return to Mills Road and her mother was the only reason she and I connected. She was then a forty-two-year-old woman, not even a divorcée since she never really married like we assumed, and I was fourteen. To say we had a lot in common is wrong on the face of it, but same knows same, one desperation calls out without speaking to another, and we became friends. In the midst of the murmur of the family crowd, the occasional dolphin-high screams of the smallest children, the chatter: *Do we have more paper plates? Mama, can I have . . . ? Cal, turn down that television; is this the last of the cake? Linda, Joyce, don't let your boys play on the stairs,* Aunt Ginny retreated to the living room, forbidden for children, with her romance novel from Goodwill and a pencil.

"Are you looking for something?" she said.

"I'll know when I find it," I said creeping my way along the back of the stiff Victorian sofa, full of shiny tasseled pillows that had to be moved to allow anyone to sit. Above the fake fireplace, my grandmother had pictures of her favorite children, her son James, a rakish knowing on his face as he stood on the tarmac on some army base in Germany, and her youngest boy, the artist (still in Denver or has he moved again?), smiling wide, a beauty in his high school graduation cap and gown. I hesitated to look directly at Aunt Ginny, convinced that seeing her face would compel me to leave.

"What are you doing in here anyway?" I said.

Aunt Ginny sighed and held up *With This Ring,* her romance, an old one judging by the ragged cover of faded and almost disappeared lovers in a posed embrace, framed by the curve of overlapping wedding rings. "I'm reading my literature."

"Those books are trash," I laughed, unable to keep the smugness out of my voice.

"That's my business."

"They're all the same book."

"Oh, so you know everything, is that how it is?"

"I never said I know everything."

"Really, I thought every twelve-year-old in the world knew it all."

"I'm fourteen, Aunt Ginny."

Aunt Ginny laughed, "Oh, excuse me, fourteen. Come back when you're thirty with a lick of sense." Aunt Ginny had clearly been asleep, and her hair was matted on one side, her face was still slack with it. She didn't look like a person with knowledge of any true thing.

"Why don't you stay home if you want to avoid everybody so bad?"

Aunt Ginny sucked her teeth in disgust but didn't answer right away, like she was considering the idea and trying to think of a real response. "I couldn't tell you," she snorted. Every week we talked, read, but mostly listened as Sunday moved along in the next room. My grandmother and her widowed sister sat at the kitchen table, their stomachs pleased and pouted in their cooking smocks, sighing with fatigue. Harold, the oldest, telling stories that ended with him righteous and victorious. "He's a dick," Aunt Ginny said, and I nodded. I had suspected as much. From the basement, the male voices rumbled, my grandfather barking proper form for the free weights, his yelps punctuated by the routine of the click of metal on metal. My mother's voice was swallowed in the clamor of women talk. Every Sunday, for months, I met Aunt Ginny in the living room as I passed by my own mama without a word. We often handled each other like we were hot around the edges, careful not to start another round of the war we both heard rumbling in the near distance. I felt my mother's sad eyes follow my back into the living room. Long years would pass before I knew to feel sorry for her.

My grandmother's house is on Mills Road, just off Highway 16, little more than a path used for years by loggers. When my mother was just a girl, she loved to listen to the saws and the pull, then catch, of the flat-headed blades in the meat of the trees. The jangle, then click, of the metal chains twisting around the logs dragging them from the woods. The trees were almost nude with most of the leaves and branches gone, the tops lopped off, headless, making them look more like skinned animals than wood. Once, when the workingmen used uncovered tractors in these hilly woods, a man hired to gather felled trees was killed, cracked to pieces by a massive pine that rushed to him, his back no obstacle to the tree's progress to the ground. The trees the men cut fall with tremendous noise, destroying without compunction or remorse the absentminded or just unlucky.

That story must have haunted my mother because every time she told it, her face glowed with the same amazement and surprise, the same awe. And though I no longer wanted to hear my mother's stories, I couldn't help but think about her standing where I stood, a girl too, schooled already in the language of last resort.

A hundred yards of grass separated the house from the rise of packed red clay above the highway. When we were children, my cousins and I threw rocks as big as eggs as hard as we could at the passing cars below, never once hearing the satisfying ping of the contact of the stone on glass or metal, a sound we reached as far as we could to catch, a sound that would break our hearts if it happened, though we believed it inevitable.

Aunt Ginny's house is only a quarter mile from my grandmother's, but lower on the hill, leaning against the downward slope of the road. You don't notice the house's lean at first, but once you see it, it's hard not to think of Aunt Ginny's house as an alive thing stubborn and willful, human enough to take on earth's most immutable laws.

In her backyard, Aunt Ginny's father had planted thick vines of muscadine grapes on wobbly looking wooden structures. You heard the vine and the contented buzzing of drunken bees before you ever rounded to the back of the house and actually saw it.

"Sounds like a giant hive," Aunt Ginny

said, "but they won't hurt you as long as you take it easy." Aunt Ginny moved to the vine, picked a fat grape, smoothed the white film like gunpowder with her thumb from the grape's skin, and took a delicate bite with her front teeth. "So good," she said. "The little ones are pretty tart, but not bad. Come on. I'm not picking for you."

I watched Aunt Ginny as long as I could, but as she expected, I inched to the vine to pick for myself.

"I'm making wine this year. I always wanted to do that," she said.

"Yeah?" I said, concentrating on the thick clusters, careful not to pinch the body of a yellow bee between my fingers. "How many grapes do we need?"

"I don't know. Enough. Let's get this pail about full and we'll quit."

"What else do you need to make wine?"

"Grapes make wine."

"If you're Jesus," I said.

"I'm getting a bucket, smart ass. Keep picking." By the time Aunt Ginny returned, my hands and mouth were full, and Aunt Ginny wasn't picking, just staring at me, the dusty bucket over her chest like a breastplate. "Do some things you want to do in your life. Hear?"

"Shut up, Aunt Ginny. God," I said, hating the lessons I was sure came to Aunt Ginny from hard experience.

"I'm serious. Don't wait around. Like sex. Do it as much as you can. I'm telling you the truth. One day, you'll look over your lifetime of being a good girl and doing all the things you were supposed to and you'll be as mad and crazy as I am."

"Okay, Aunt Ginny, I'll have sex with everybody I know, even dogs. Will that make you happy?"

"You've got a filthy mouth on you," Aunt Ginny said as she shook the grapes to settle them. I was embarrassed at my joke. But it wasn't that bad, maybe stupid, but any other time Aunt Ginny would get it.

"Did you see my daddy?" she said, pointing to the house. "In mama's room." Aunt Ginny's glimpse of her daddy had changed her mood. I don't know if it's possible to hate someone you've never met, but I hated her daddy. But I wouldn't look. If I saw him in the window then every other face with his same turn of jaw, every hungry-looking man cupping his rusty knuckles to keep the match flame alive, sparing it from the air, scratching his leg with the back of his dirty shoe, in Denver, Kansas City, Ohio, Winston-Salem, or even in my dinky small town would forever move me to hate.

27

Some of the dead you feel like warmth, their presence a consolation, or so I've heard. My only experience with the dead was with my father's mother, her presence the intensity of a clenched fist. She'd never forgiven me for coming into the world two weeks before she died. But I knew from the cold rage coming off of Aunt Ginny that her daddy's presence was no comfort to anybody. "Yeah," I muttered, my mouth full of grapes, making my lips pucker with juice. I knew enough about Aunt Ginny's father to fear even the flutter of a panel of curtain he moved. I turned my back so Aunt Ginny's father couldn't see my face either. "Tell him to leave," I said.

Aunt Ginny dropped her handful of grapes in the pail one at a time; the soft thuds seemed a comfort. She chuckled, "Are you used to things being easy?"

A few weeks later, Aunt Ginny waited for me outside my grandmother's house, leaning on her Buick, reading. "Hey Bebe. Roger," she nodded to my parents. "You want to go to the store?" I was already halfway in the car before my mother could answer. "Bebe, you don't care, do you?" Aunt Ginny asked, her hand on the door handle.

My mother hesitated, tried to catch my eye as both a warning and a talisman against harm. I wouldn't meet her stare. "Come right back," Mama said.

Aunt Ginny reached across the bench seat and tossed a sweater, some shoes, and a couple books to the back. "Get in. We've got to hurry," Aunt Ginny said too loudly, mostly for my mother's benefit. Once on the dusty road, Aunt Ginny rolled her eyes to me. "*My* mother said bring back an onion," she said and we both laughed at our mothers and their worthless concern like the two of us were girls together.

"Where are we going?"

"Do you care?" Aunt Ginny rolled down her window, letting the air flip her curls in every direction.

"Not really." I picked up one of Aunt Ginny's books from the floorboard. Everywhere Aunt Ginny went, every room of her house, my grandmother's, and now obviously her car, she left these romances scattered like she molted them. I read aloud: *Her hair flowed and swirled gloriously like honey against the smooth silk of the lavender sheet. Am I beautiful? she whispered. Yes, yes, a thousand times yes, he said caressing the down of her perfect cheek.* "Man, how do you read this?"

29

"Just wait, little girl. You're going to feel just like that some day. Mark my words. Then don't come to me with none of this, 'But, Aunt Ginny, I love him. But Aunt Ginny, he's my everything.' "

"Oh, God, if I ever say, 'He's my everything,' I want you to kill me."

"Not if, when. When, little girl."

"Yeah, okay, we'll see," I said pleased to be talking about my future romantic life, even my refusal of it making that shadow world possible and even legitimate. "What do you need from the store, anyway?"

"Nothing. Just felt like taking a drive."

We turned on to a dirt road, barely big enough for one good-sized car, to a brick ranch house, tiny by today's standards. Not like the new houses that have sprouted up everywhere with extra rooms nobody enters that, more often than not, go unused, leaving behind little more than the deflated sense of the wrong promises fulfilled. But this was a starting-out place that people were happy to start with years ago (this year the hardwood floors, next year the addition), full of possibility. The house didn't look lived in. Not that it wasn't neat or was unkempt, but it was a house without intention; even the grass was filled in with lush green clumps here or there, but bald as sand in the next patch. Aunt Ginny killed the engine and we waited.

"Whose house is this? Gerald's?"

Aunt Ginny nodded her head.

"Are we getting out?"

"I don't think so," Aunt Ginny said.

"He'll see us. You know that, don't you?"

Ginny rolled her window all the way up. "Lock your door," she said. "He'll come out in a minute."

"What are we doing here?"

"You want to meet your Uncle Gerald, don't you?"

"I've seen him plenty of times," I whined.

Gerald poked his head out the door. I thought he might be annoyed or even that his face would flash with anger, but he didn't look surprised. "Ya'll coming in?" he yelled. In those days, I scrutinized every aspect of a person's appearance and I knew all there was to know about Gerald's clothed body, but he looked kinder outside of my grandmother's house. His feet were bare and flat like snowshoes, and he wore a T-shirt oversized to accommodate his belly that made him look square and wide as a freezer. "Come on, if you're coming," he said.

"Let's go," Aunt Ginny grabbed my hand.

31

"Is it all right?" she said. Aunt Ginny's desperation embarrassed me, but I couldn't let her see that I wanted to please her.

"We're here now," I sighed.

"Who is this?" Gerald said as if he suspected a trick.

"She's my niece, Gerald. Act like you've got some sense."

"I didn't say nothing." Gerald turned to go back inside. "How you doing?" he said over his shoulder. Aunt Ginny smiled at me like I had passed some test. "Ya'll want cake? My sister brought over some coconut cake."

Gerald's house was dark, with mahogany paneling and floors, curtains pulled together like a modest lady's towel on her bosom, each room pinched with every door possible closed to the visitor's eye. Gerald led us to his sparse living room with only a dirty plaid chair, a low-riding sofa to match Heimlich-maneuvered against the room's longest wall, and a console television stacked with years of *Ebony* magazines.

"I set up my poker games in here," Gerald grinned. "We're not fancy."

"It's nice," I said, embarrassed that Gerald had to explain.

"You've got good timing, Ginny. I'm in the middle of the game."

Aunt Ginny shifted on her feet like she was embarrassed.

Gerald quickly added, "The Redskins will choke up anyway. They always do. Especially if I have some money on it." Aunt Ginny giggled and accepted his apology, as pleased as if Gerald had said something charming.

"You can turn the dial, but I don't get but two channels down here," Gerald said to me.

"Where are you going?"

"We're going to talk a minute," Aunt Ginny said. "Will you be all right?"

"Talk?"

"Just right there," Aunt Ginny said as she motioned to the bedroom, an uncharacteristic softness in her voice. "Just a minute."

I rolled my eyes at Aunt Ginny. What did she want me to do?

The other channel on Gerald's television came in only weakly, a dim pulse. Gerald had been generous about getting two channels, but the other station was just another football game anyway. I turned up the volume to cover the mumble from the next room. If I'd been thinking I could have gotten one of Aunt Ginny's romances, but I didn't think of it. I was alone and uncomfortable and feeling like my mother who hated being alone. My mother imagined that the rest of the world was invited to a great party with laughing people, too swaddled and secure to experience the abjection of the lonely. Her invitation never arrived. Though for years, I watched her stare out the window, a withering in her eyes, a sad turn on her already frowned lips. I was determined to duck and dodge loneliness, and when that didn't work, I begged it away. Still, loneliness managed to find me. Though I wasn't used to feeling it around Aunt Ginny.

The living room was about as inviting as a hypodermic needle, but the outside didn't look much better. Above the largest couch was a picture window like a large television screen, but the show was pines straight as soldiers in a dark copse across the road. If I explored those woods, like the muscled and strong nature girls I envied, would I find a graying bone sticking from the underbrush of pine needles or a swarm of insects crawling over each other like the bubbles in boiling water? I believed I would.

I will feel this way again. In less than two years, I will be sixteen with my best friend in her grandmother's house, when her boyfriend will emerge from the kitchen with an ancient rubber from his wallet filled to bursting with water, his face all teeth and light as he offers it to us, the reservoir tip of the condom pointing hard and up like a nipple. My best friend will betray me by thinking this hilarious.

In that very moment, Aunt Ginny will come to me with the completeness of plunging into a tunnel, and I will remember that day two years before when Aunt Ginny and Gerald are together, and I am only a room away. I will see them as clear as an honest memory: Aunt Ginny and Gerald intertwined. She grips his back, her fingers dimpling his fatty flesh, his face lovely now in its proximity to hers. I know it does not come to mind, the bulge of his body or even her own ungainly proportions, but she will concentrate on his fingers and knees, smooth baby skin of his ear, the scrub of his kinky hair on her legs. Lazarus died twice. The second time for good. Not every miracle lasts. And I will breathe a few choking sighs (sighs my friend will mistake for muffled laughter) glad at last that Aunt Ginny brought me with her to Gerald's to share with her as much as I could the biggest and most complicated miracle of her life.

A large green car rolled into the driveway behind the Buick, looking like a parade float, with the back end of it extended into the road. I was angry with Aunt Ginny, but I didn't want her humiliated and ran to get to the front porch before whoever was in that car tried to come into the house.

"Hey," the woman yelled.

"Hey."

"Where's Gerald? Is he here?"

I looked to the door not sure what to say. "Yeah. I think so."

"I'm his sister. They call me Sister. I know he's here. Tell him to come out."

"He's busy."

"Busy? You a Harshaw? You look just like them with them chinky eyes. Is Ginny Harshaw in there?" Sister got out of her car and moved quickly to the house. "She's in there sure enough. Stupid, stupid ass. Not Ginny, baby. My brother. How long they been at it?"

"I didn't time them."

"Don't you get attitude in your voice. I'm just asking a question. You know as well as I do what's going on." Sister leaned her skinny frame against the closed door of

Gerald's house. Her face was Gerald's, the same big eyes and round jolly cheeks. "If he's like any man I know, we shouldn't be waiting out here but a minute," Sister giggled, but I was years from understanding that joke. Besides, I was annoyed that she had indirectly insulted Aunt Ginny.

"Gerald's nobody's prize," I said.

Sister laughed, "Who said anything about all that? I'm just saying the both of them need to start acting like grown people. Gerald ain't got sense. I know it. I'm by myself, and you don't see me acting a fool all the time, sneaking around like a child. If you want a woman, get one. Damn. I'd rather he find the Lord. You won't catch me listening to those Jewish fables, but they do some people a whole lot of good."

Sister stuck her head in the house but appeared to change her mind and didn't go inside. "Look at you standing out here looking right lonesome."

"Nowhere else to be," I said, sounding more pitiful than I meant.

"You hungry?"

"I'm all right."

"You'd say that, wouldn't you? My house is on the next road. I've got food cooked if you're hungry."

"I'm all right."

37

"Your Aunt Ginny is not studying you right now. Come on, I'll take you to the store then. There's the Run In a minute from here. You can get a bar of candy or soda."

"Can you take me to my grandmother's?"

Sister paused and looked at her watch but shook her head, like the ticking hands on the face had made her decision for her.

"This ain't a Yellow Cab," Sister laughed. "By the time we get back, your Aunt Ginny will be ready for you."

Sister and I pulled up to a small box of a store. "Here's a dollar," she said.

But I had a couple of dollars in a sweated wad in my pocket. "No, thanks," I said. Sister returned her dollar to her purse, shrugged her shoulders, a whatever-you-want expression on her face.

Run In was only big enough for a couple of rows of candy, chips, soup, and cola, the few toiletries and motor oil covered in a film of dust.

An older man, maybe as old as twenty, sat on a wooden stool behind the counter talking to a boy I had seen at school lurking in the smoking section beside the basketball court. The clerk nodded hello to me, barely letting his gaze land on my face. I was a child to him, invisible and unimportant.

"I've never seen you in here," the boy from school said. I didn't realize that he'd ever seen me anywhere since he'd never before raised his hand in greeting or looked directly at my face. I grabbed the nearest candy bar, Chunky, a thick kind with nuts and raisins I hated, and an orange soda and brought them to the counter.

"We'll let you stay with us," the boy said, winking at the clerk. "You want to give us a try?" he whispered as he leaned toward me. "We'll be sweet to you." The clerk laughed but kept his seat, his rough fingers tickling my palm with the change from the dollar. I wanted to stay and let something more significant happen to me, an event I would savor in the retelling. But even then, I knew that staying could never be the right choice. I wanted to say something sassy and sure, but instead I threw the soda close to the boy's feet, hoping to hear the soda explode out like a hydrant all over the boy's shoes. Though the can hissed, it did not pop open but rolled like a loyal dog to the boy's feet. "What the hell is wrong with you?" I heard at my back as I wiped my eyes and retreated to the door. "Is she crazy?"

Aunt Ginny and Gerald were already outside when we got back. I expected to see visible relief on Aunt Ginny's face as I appeared, or at least an acknowledgment, but neither she nor Gerald did more than glance up at us for the briefest moment before returning to their conversation.

Sister honked her horn as she pulled out of the driveway. "Stupid ass," she yelled to Gerald, hoping he would have the decency to show at least a little shame.

"Ginny, I'm tired of this shit," Gerald said, picking his hair straight up with the pick he kept in the back of his fro. "Goddammit," he said, but he sounded like he might cry.

"Aunt Ginny, let's go," I said.

"I'm coming."

"Let's go now."

"I'll see you," Aunt Ginny said as she turned her back to Gerald and walked the few steps to the car.

"What are you waiting on?" I said. Gerald watched us, his ugly toes exposed and pleading. I kicked the dashboard of the Buick, leaving the footprint of my shoe on the burgundy vinyl. "Did you even know I was gone?"

"I don't know. Let me think," Aunt Ginny said, her head on the steering wheel.

"Just go."

Aunt Ginny started the car, though we

still didn't move.

"Go on then. I don't want you," Gerald yelled, his voice cracking like a growing boy's. Aunt Ginny pretended not to have heard.

I rolled down my window, leaned as far out the car as I could. "You go straight to hell," I screamed.

"Don't, don't," Aunt Ginny pulled on my arm, coaxed me back down into the car. To this day, I'm not sure if she was protecting him or me. Gerald said nothing. In fact, the three of us sat, the way people do, when they wait for the life-changing moment to come.

"I used to really love him," Aunt Ginny said.

Gerald finally turned around and went back inside his house. At any minute I was sure he would return with a flower, a baseball bat, with a love poem or grenade, but he didn't come back at all.

"Aunt Ginny, go," I said.

"He's coming back," Aunt Ginny said, though she backed the car from the drive, turned her head to the dusty road. It would be years, but just as Aunt Ginny predicted, I would feel this kind of love for myself, desperate, stupid, the way Aunt Ginny did or the ways I hoped my parents did (though, in fact, I knew better), and though this day was my first trek on love's complex terrain, I knew only a fool would doubt that Aunt Ginny loved Gerald still.

My family arrived at my grandmother's early the next Sunday. Though the front door opened many times, Aunt Ginny did not come. I didn't get to listen to the sounds of the house, with her, or see her pretzel her long legs under her body as she read her trashy book about white people in rich implausible adventures. Just before dark, I walked to her house to the green paint glowing the color of forgetting in the fading light. I could hear her waiting inside, her tense holding out behind the door. "Aunt Ginny, let me in," I yelled. I was fourteen and in my worst, most painful year. I wanted to tell someone about it, confess it all, but there was no one, and worse than that, there was nothing to tell. But still I made a vow that when my own daughter is fourteen, I will fill the gap for her. I will not let her flounder disconnected and alone. And I believe I would have followed through on that promise. I know it to be true. But although I felt her in quick flashes of being in my belly over the years, she was just as quickly gone. It would be years before I would finally accept that she would never arrive.

In the car, the very next Sunday, my father made his usual speech full of the dread of his in-laws, people who forever thought him too common. "Seven o'clock. No later, I mean it, Bebe." But my mother had decided that her life amounted to these Sundays. She would stay as long as she pleased.

I was sure Aunt Ginny would not be at my grandmother's, but there she was, in the kitchen at the table, cutting herself a huge slab of dense chocolate cake. "There's my girl," she said. "Come help me eat this."

So much happened in the coming weeks. The grapes we picked turned to wine by themselves, the bucket forgotten and abandoned outside to become crunchy with insects and drowned bees. A boy I considered falling in love with rammed his hand between my legs on the bus, fluttered his dirty fingers in my lap while his friends hooted like sports fans. For a quick sweet moment, I thought that meant I was desired. And late one Saturday night, the phone rang long and lonesome, not the discordant ring of the wrong number, or the quick bright ring of my mother's sisters, but the drawn-out moan of bad news. Aunt Ginny was in the hospital unconscious from a bottle of pills. If her mother hadn't come back early for the forgotten thing on the kitchen table, Aunt Ginny would be dead.

"I'm going to the hospital." My mother wrapped the stretched yellow cord of the telephone around her hand. "Come on, go with me?"

I did want to go, but I was more afraid than I'd ever been. For weeks my mother and I had spoken in the language of long pauses and slammed doors. We tried as much as we knew how, but the eye of whatever was passing over us had moved on, and we were in the storm of it. How can I tell you how hard it is to want not to love your mother? How much and in how many ways I would struggle not to let her know that anything she says means a damn to me. "Why is Aunt Ginny's sister buried in their yard?" I said, my voice trembling.

"You listen to me," my mother said, her face rabid with anger and pain, "your Aunt Ginny is sick. You're old enough to understand." My mother sighed, holding the top of her head like it might fly off.

"I don't like liars," I said.

My mother's face dropped, with shock, but also with despair.

"It's not even her sister, is it?" I taunted, knowing the truth but not yet realizing how dangerous and insignificant the truth is in a life.

"We don't have time for this. Let's go," she said, talking slowly like she was talking to an incompetent. My mother was trying hard not to hate me. I knew it, and I blamed her, though I hated me, too. The only difference between us was she could forgive me. We had been close friends for years, better than friends, but in that moment and many like it, neither of us understood that we would be friends again.

"I'll go when I get ready," I said, careful to stay just out of range of her arm.

"You make me sick," she said as she snatched her pocketbook from the table, jingled her keys for comfort. "Suit yourself. But you always do, don't you?"

The next Sunday at my grandmother's, two days after the funeral, the mood was quiet. At least for a while. Aunt Ginny's story was played over and over: *her hair, you should have seen it. That Gerald, he's to blame. A shame, a shame. Did you see him at the funeral crying, looking as pitiful and ignored as an ugly child?* He should cry, we all agreed. But Aunt Ginny's mother didn't blame Gerald. All day long and for the rest of her life she'd find a way to insert in conversation that Aunt Ginny died of pneumonia. She told that lie so many times, her face as clear and untroubled as a turnip, she finally convinced herself. And in no time at all, two hours, three, we ate, became many, generations in the small rooms of my grandmother's house, and we closed over the hole Ginny's passing made — a stone dropped into a lake.

It has been years, nearly twenty, since Aunt Ginny lived in that old house on Mills Road, a gravel road now with fine gray dust from pulverized rock in layers over the red clay of my childhood. Now my cousin Mavis and her kids live there, but they will go soon. Nobody stays in that house long. Nothing works right in the old place, and newer is better, we all know that. I was thirty-three, old as Jesus, and had just buried my mother, the last time I went inside.

My mother, Bebe Marilyn Harshaw Thomas, had always said that she wouldn't live to be old, and she was right. It is a cliché to say she was right about a lot of things. It is also true. The old green house was seemingly stuck in the same stage of decay it had been in twenty years ago when Aunt Ginny invited me in. Aunt Ginny's room was the room Mavis' daughter shared with her toddler brother, the little boy too young to have any opinion, so Aunt Ginny's old room was still a girl's room.

Though Mavis' child plastered the wall with Disney and television cartoon characters, all I could still see were Aunt Ginny's music boxes in a row on her dresser, dozens of fraying romances, her record player with the handled carrying box, the neat stack of her 45s we danced to one afternoon, until we got tired of her heavy jumping, skipping the needle, her twin bed covered in a white cotton bedspread like a corpse, and in the closet, heaps of clothes Aunt Ginny could scoop up in a hurry, if somebody ever waited for her in the driveway again.

And her father. Still there. But not after that day. I would stay until he came in the room, as long as it took, until I felt him vibrate on the air. He would not be staring over a child this time. That day he would face me, a woman who never desired to love him. A woman, sure she'd lost for the second and final time, the person in the world who loved her most. You don't get too many people who love you like that. For them, I would force him out of that house for good. I would scream at him, fight him if it came to that. For Aunt Ginny, still and forever forty-two. For my mother, whom I would never see again in this life but would feel when I woke every morning, her palm warm on my forehead. "You have to get up," she'd whisper, and I'd jerk awake, eager to follow her voice.

"Get out, get out, out, out," I screamed. I'd make him hear it until my throat was raw and sore. And he would. May God strike me dead if I lie, but before I left that house for good, I heard his retreating steps, the mincing steps of a coward. I heard the creak of the front door, the draft, colder than it should have been. I feel it still. Seconds before the front door slammed, shaking the frame, final as an axe blade, closed and closed.

IF YOU HIT RANDOLPH COUNTY, YOU'VE GONE TOO FAR

The first time my brother got out of county jail, we rejoiced. The sight of him, stupid grin, without orange coveralls, made us all feel better, like we had been given a reprieve — a pardon? And now we could all make good. Nobody said this. In my family we never say anything that means anything, just *nothing, nothing, nothing* all the time — the very reason we are such bastards and idiots in the world. But you could tell by the way we hugged him, took him to the new Sizzler on franchise row in Randolph County. How we let him order what he wanted, the big steak, if he could eat it, with the dessert bar, including ice cream, anything. Even his girl, Renee, most of the reason he had to sit up in jail anyway, was there, letting Greg feed her tossed salad, not a finger food to my mind, with his dirty hands and nails. We pretended that we didn't notice that they were practically doing it all over the plastic

49

upholstery booth. We were just glad. He was one of us again. And as sorry as that has turned out to be, that is all we have.

I wasn't for sure we'd even be able to get him out of jail in the first place. Somebody had to put up bail, mortgage a house, or come into money none of us had ever seen, much less held long in our hands, except maybe at tax time or gambling. Maybe. Even the Christmas bonus Daddy got from the furniture factory was just a few hundred dollars at the most. None of us, probably not all of us put together, could work up that kind of money on the spot. Bond was 100,000 and ten percent is still 10,000. I don't know what 10,000 means. But I come in peace. Daddy was the one who signed over his house, put his own X on the line on the long shot that my brother was good for it.

Greg tried to ignore me. I was right across from his ignorant girlfriend — no way he couldn't see me in the curved booth, but he was steadily trying. Shifting his head from Daddy beside me, to Mark the oldest on my other side, to our airhead little sister Shelia next to his girlfriend. How stupid he looked tipping his chin up and over my face to look at everybody else. I shouldn't blame him. Wasn't I the one who said let him stay in there? Wasn't I sure he should learn a lesson? Selling crack rock. And for what? To get skinny-assed Renee another pair of gold-hoop earrings? Greg's lost his mind. Eddie Bailey, the policeman who arrested Greg, said he might get a year. A year! That scared us. Me, Daddy, Mark all sat in Eddie Bailey's office at the police station, dumb as a load of knees, awestruck and stupid like Eddie Bailey had just started speaking in tongues.

Most likely Greg won't get the whole time. A first offense like this. The best part is they didn't find any drugs on him. Greg had sense enough to throw the crack rocks behind him as he ran and let them scatter in the gravel on the shoulder of Honeysuckle Road. What they didn't find on his body, they couldn't prove was his.

"Daddy, I'm going to get a job at the plant Monday. They hiring, right?"

Daddy wouldn't look at Greg but stared into the overdone macaroni and cheese, stirred the mound of purple beets into the pasta.

"I don't know, Greg. Things are getting tight. I might have my own hours cut here in a minute." Daddy shoveled a hunk of the beets and macaroni pink and slippery from beet juice into his mouth. Disgusting. If you asked him, he'd tell you the food gets mixed up in your stomach anyway. Nobody could stand to see him eat. I do have to give him some credit for trying to soften the blow. The truth was that Daddy didn't want Greg coming to the plant, making like everything's a big game, the way he does, messing up the wood they use for the expensive furniture, flirting with the old white women who worked in the reception area. Greg was too silly to realize that the women saw him as a lowlife and a thug and half-smiled to his face but kicked their purses farther under the desk when they saw him coming. Greg couldn't see beyond his own fool self. He'd never be able to suck it all up like Daddy did and stand at his station and do the job without feeling like a punk or a Tom. I give him a week at the plant, tops.

"You ought to think about acting like somebody," I said, stuffing an oversized cherry tomato in my mouth, the sour juice gushing on my lips.

Greg did look at me then and pointed his bony finger in my face. "It ain't even worth it," he laughed to Renee, like I'd made a joke, but there was nothing about laughing in his eyes. Renee, as usual, had nothing to say, but shifted her shoulder away from me like she smelled something sour in my direction.

"What is worth it?" I said and folded my arms across my chest. I thought the move made me look like I'd made a decision I was bound to stick to. At the time, I thought I had him. I thought it was a good line, very lawyer-like, like the last words on *Perry Mason* that's so good it gets repeated. "What is worth it, Greg? What is worth it?" Now I'm not so sure. I should have said something sweeter. Always start with love. That's what our grandmother says. Start with love, and when it fails, like it will, knock the hell out of the truth.

I care. I do. I went to see him at the jailhouse, which is more than Renee did. And none of that was a bit easy. If you are picturing Paul Newman or Denzel or some other fine man inside a 5 × 7 behind a technicality or mistake, throw that piece of Hollywood nothing out your head. There's nobody there but sad types, con artists, dope dealers, beaters, stealers, and good boys, poor, young looking, young being, just on the verge of unreachable. Greg was none of these. Well, technically he was a dope dealer because he sold some dope, but that mess wasn't his life. Someday I'm going to sit Greg down and tell him that nothing I've said comes from a bad place. I'm going to say, I'm just concerned, like the clean-looking white people do on television.

Greg slid the almost empty salad bowl to the end of the table with the other dirty dishes. "I haven't had good salad like that in a long time," he said.

Greg could enjoy some wilted lettuce and too much Russian dressing like he had something. He could be okay no matter what. He took that after Daddy, that calmness. One time Mama screamed at Daddy from the stands at a softball game. "Hit a home run or don't come home," she said. Everybody laughed like crazy, all of Daddy's friends, their wives and children, all in on the joke. None of that made Daddy mad or made him curl up on himself in shame. He just shrugged his shoulders and was as surprised and happy as anybody when he hit his only over-the-fence ball of the whole season.

"Round two," Greg said, grabbing Renee's hand in his. He kissed her forehead lightly like she was a precious thing, a dyed Easter chick in his cupped hand.

"How romantic," I said, but nobody laughed.

"Let the boy live," Mark said, cleaning the space between his two front teeth with his straw. Like a straw was supposed to be used for mouth hygiene, like his thirty-year-old mouth was a prayer book. He never even lived with us when we were little, just showed up one day and his mama said he wasn't her problem anymore. Now, Mark's taken over the whole family.

"He's all right," Mark said.

"Look here, I'm just calling it like I see it. The boy didn't just come home from Iraq." I tossed my paper napkin into my still full salad bowl. "I'm just trying to be realistic."

Shelia as usual was quiet, signaling with her eyes that she agreed with everything Mark said. You'd think being a girl and just two years younger that she'd be on my side. But I can't remember a day, a time, a single minute in life when Shelia Eileen ever looked over the fence to my side. Shelia was easy with people like Greg. That made me crazier than anything. I got the fight honest from my mother. I couldn't think about Mama without the sight of her yelling, her usually pretty face ugly and twisted like a Halloween mask. Daddy used to tell this story about Mama coming into the plant in the back way carrying her sewing machine. Mama was a little thing, with thin arms like sticks, and I can just see her huffing and puffing from lugging around that heavy machine. Soon as she got in front of Daddy's station, she flung that thing as hard and as far as she could onto the concrete floor. The metal guts went skidding all over the place, and the hard plastic face of it got split in two pieces. "You won't be moving my shit again, will you?" she'd said. People at the plant called Daddy Singer for years over that. Every once and a while somebody still will. But I didn't feel sorry for Daddy. Every time I heard the story, I felt with Mama, got mad as hell right with her. Mad as she must have been all those years ago, like no time and a million decisions hadn't filled the space of those twenty-five years since that day.

"Well, if nobody cares, I'm going to get something to eat," I rolled my eyes at Shelia. I could go off, but I was going to be the bigger person today and just walk away.

Daddy got up from the booth to let me out. "Go on then, Dee," Daddy waved his hand like an impatient crossing guard as I struggled out of the skinny booth. It ain't easy to look like a hero bouncing your weight across a squeaking plastic seat.

The food bar was depressing, like every one you've ever seen. A big blob of mashed potatoes straight from the box, green beans in rusty water, spongy meatloaf covered in ketchup, carrots, chicken wings, and a mound of fried chicken in a large metal bin, the few pieces of breast meat hidden in a whole chicken farm of legs and thighs.

I grabbed one of the chicken legs, some corn, as many of the green beans as I could stomach. I couldn't let Mark and Shelia cut their eyes to my full plate, both thinking that the mystery of the big ass was finally solved.

An African woman and her little girl were on the other side of the bar. They were in American clothes, but you can spot an African anywhere. They always look peaceful, like they know what's going on more than you do. The woman's little girl had a head full of fake hair braided into about a dozen shoulder length plaits; each one had either a small green or red bow.

"Don't stick your fingers in the corn," she said, but when she pronounced it, it sounded like cairn. The little girl looked up quickly at me, embarrassed that I saw her, and put both hands behind her back. I grinned at her. This slop should tempt somebody.

The African woman loaded her plate with food, going through the bar like somebody was going to tell her to stop at any minute and she had to get all she wanted or go home. The woman dipped a slotted spoon into the pinto beans, carefully stacking them to the side of her plate beside a mound of yellow cabbage, like the final piece of her sculpture. She must not eat like this all the time. Her body was lean, skinny even, and flat as a twelve-year-old boy's. Her dark brown skin was as clear and smooth as cowhide. I bet she was beautiful back where she was from. I wonder if she's surprised that even the black people here don't get it.

This girl I work with whose sister-in-law was from somewhere in Africa said the mothers over there have to keep their babies in long-legged cribs, each foot of the furniture in a plate of gas. I thought it was some kind of voodoo thing, but she said they had to keep the fire ants away from the babies. I wanted to ask the woman if she had to keep her little girl in one of those cribs, but she wouldn't look over the food bins to me. Besides, sometimes Africans are touchy.

I got back to the table last and had to sit at the end of the booth beside Daddy. The rest of them had plates like the African woman's, plates that looked like they'd needed help carrying.

"Boring as hell," Greg said. "That's the worst part of it. It was all right. Can make a man out of you, though. Quick." Greg was talking like he'd done some real time and not just laid up in the jail for just under two weeks. Still, he was the only one of us to ever spend any time in lock up at all. I wanted to ask him questions, just the things you wonder, showers and eating, what it feels like to hear the doors close and lock, but I couldn't ask about any of that. I was proud not to know.

"There was this guy in there, crazy," Greg whistled. "He should have been in a hospital or something, but they didn't give a damn."

"I believe that's Donna Perkins' boy," Daddy said.

"No, it wasn't Dougie. I know Dougie. If you talk to him a little bit, you can settle Dougie down. No, this was a little guy, a kid, too. A screamer," Greg laughed. "It's not funny. I'm not laughing at him. But just as soon as the lights went, he'd get started. You'd have thought somebody was killing him." Greg ate a few bites of his mashed potatoes, his eyes on the plate. Nobody knew what to say. "Carl Banner's back in," Greg said between bites.

At least three years ago, Shelia spent some time with dumb-as-a-rock Carl Banner. Until he started running with this white girl Greg knew from high school. When Shelia found out, she flopped around the house for days, all her junk and stank covers in a ball on the couch. I don't think she turned the television off for a week. Greg stopped chewing and stared at Shelia. You could tell he was worried that he hurt her feelings. But Shelia didn't suck in her breath, or let her eyes well up or anything, but kept on eating her pork and gravy.

Nobody cared what I thought. I might as well have been a piece of furniture, a cheap restaurant chair or one of these plastic checkered tablecloths these Sizzler people ought to be ashamed of (next thing they'll be making us wear bibs). Like my Daddy's friend Hubey always says when he's talking about lost causes, "I got mad yesterday and didn't nobody care." Nobody did. I took apart the chicken leg with my fork and chewed tiny bites to make it last. I couldn't let them see me run out of food and just be sitting there with nothing to do or say.

"Look here," Mark said. "Come by the house tonight, and I'll make you a tape."

Mark was all the time talking about his house, which wasn't a house at all but a double-wide trailer at the top of the hill. Mark wasted hours making improvements to it. You would have thought he lived in a castle the way he talked. You would have thought that rusty old mess was all he ever

60

wanted. Serena, Mark's longtime girlfriend, was just as bad. She decorated every open inch of the place with ruffles and white baby dolls. In my more generous moments, I had to admit it did look sweet.

"Serena won't be at work tonight. She'd like to see you."

"I can do that," Greg grinned.

You can't take back worry. You can't. But if you could, I would have sucked up every second I spent thinking about Greg in that cell. Every second I wondered if he was all right. I would have taken my visit back. That wasn't nothing. Jail is a scary place for decent people. Even the Randolph County jail, and it's new. Gray walls, gray floors, gray everything. You walk in the door to the visitor's area, and you feel like you're on the way to lockup yourself. At the end of the hall is a shoebox-sized opening in a bulletproof cubby big enough for one person to sit in. I had six pairs of underwear to give to Greg, Right Guard deodorant, a razor, some candy in a big bag, Oreos, undershirts from the Family Thrift, and socks. I knew he wouldn't read, not even a magazine, so I didn't bother. I thought for a long minute about bringing the Bible, but Greg wouldn't touch it. I wouldn't either, at least I didn't think I would, but I didn't want to be

61

responsible for him turning into a Holy Roller, or worse, a Black Muslim.

"I'm here to see Greg Perkins, please. I've got some stuff for him." I tried to sound cultured like I didn't come to these places on a regular basis, like I was a notch above the whole thing. I could only see the woman's eyes and the fluff of her hair resting on her brown forehead. The sign clearly says that you can give inmates only three pairs of underwear, no socks, no treats, but sometimes, my Uncle Jerry claimed, if you caught the right woman on the right day, she would take pity on you and make sure that your loved one got some of the things you left. Sharon Alexander was on tonight. She knew me, at least she knew Daddy. She might let the extra underwear slide.

"Honey, you can't leave nothing but the BVDs. Didn't your daddy tell you that?"

"Yes, ma'am, he did, but I thought since I wouldn't be back in town until the weekend, I could leave them." I didn't tell Miss Sharon that I just lived twenty minutes away in Harmony. She probably guessed anyway. She's probably heard every lie, every half-truth and weak-assed story there is.

I could see Sharon's eyebrow arch up, but I couldn't tell if she was laughing or irritated. Could go either way.

"Put the deodorant and things under the socks, the underwear on top. I might have to have those Oreos for myself."

"Thank you, Miss Sharon," I said. I meant it. Greg can get deodorant and those things from vending machines — expensive toothpaste — but how nice of Sharon not to make us, at least not entirely. Who would have thought I'd need a friend in such a lowdown place?

"How's your daddy?"

"He's fine. The same as usual, I guess."

"You tell him Sharon Alexander said hey."

"I will, ma'am," I said, though I was sure I would forget until the unhappy time I saw Sharon at this jail again.

"You want me to tell them to bring him on up?" Sharon asked.

I'd meant to come just too late for visiting hours. I had already planned to tell anybody who asked that I'd tried but came at the wrong time. *Just missed him,* I'd say and twist my lips into a sad shape. "Yes, ma'am, if you could."

"It's Greg, right."

"Greg James Perkins."

Sharon buzzed open the door to the visitors' area. Two women, by their looks sisters, were already sitting in the visitors' chairs. Both women had blonde hair dyed the color of straw, their fatty arms dimpled and exposed in tank tops. The woman closest to me looked up and smiled, like we are in it together. I looked away.

The room was small, nothing like the prison rooms you see on television. Of course, this was just a little county jail, used to drunks and beaters. The big-ticket criminals don't hang around with these babies but grow up to the hardcore places as fast as they can move them. There were four booths, separated by a thick plastic shield. Each one of them was hardly bigger than a phone booth, with a chair on the visitor's side and one on the prisoner's side. The big plastic windows made me think we were all here to see newborn babies. I wished it was so. This room might be the most depressing place I've ever been in, except for the nights I spent on the reclining chair in the hospital with Mama Lou listening to her moan *I'm so sorry* in her sleep. We don't have long to wait before the door opens into the little room.

"Donny," one of the sisters said, excited to see the scraggly man come in. "You lost weight."

"I coulda told you that. I eat out of the vending machine. I'm trying to tell you."

"Well, you ought to at least try to eat what

they've got. You can't live off of Snickers and popcorn," the other sister said, but in her tone is play, like they are used to having this conversation, plastic shield between them or not.

"Did you tell J.B. to fertilize my yard? If you don't tell him in the next few days, won't be no need," Danny said, his face predicting the answer from his sisters.

"You're gonna stop telling me that. I told J.B. thirty times, I can't help if he does it or not."

"If I get out of here and see a patchy yard, you and you," Danny looked from one sister to the other, "both of ya'll will be planting sod, you hear?"

Both women laughed at the man who looked like their brother. His pointed finger no threat.

"Hey, Dee," Greg said as he entered the room. He sounded fine but looked scared. I know enough about him to see the stiff way he carried his body and know. His hair wasn't combed, wasn't the glistening waves he loved to slick back like a fifties singer, but high and dirty, the curl picked out and straight up in the air. I might could have held it together if he'd been allowed anything to wear but that orange jumpsuit. That and the nasty hair broke up something hard and steady in me.

"Hey, Greg. You okay?" I said, but I'm not sure if I say it out loud.

"Is Daddy getting me out?"

"I don't know. It's a lot of money."

Greg laughed, "I did it this time, didn't I?"

"Are you eating anything? Do you have enough to eat?"

"I'm all right."

"Is the food all right?"

"Is anybody with you Dee?"

"I left some underwear and things like that."

"Dee, listen," Greg leaned close to the plastic partition, his eyes yellow with sleep, a panic in the set of his eyebrows. "Is anybody coming?"

A long time ago, before Mark showed up at the house when it was just me, Shelia, and Greg, our mother came back to us. We got off the bus at the top of the road, walked in the kitchen, and there she was. It had been a year or more since we'd seen her last, but you wouldn't know it.

"My babies," Mama said, drawing us to her with her arms. Greg was the first one to wrap himself to her chest, but we all followed. Daddy was there too, his work clothes still on, standing in the hallway watching Mama like she was something good to eat.

The next morning, none of us knew what to expect, and it felt like Christmas except in reverse since all of us were ready to be robbed of the best thing we had. But there she was, watching television in the living room, her bare toes hidden between the cushions of scratchy couch.

"Are we going to school?" I said.

"Don't you always go to school?" Mama laughed. I was about to cry until she motioned me to her, held my face in her two hands, and I forgot to be ashamed. "You tell me what you want for dinner."

At four o'clock we ran from off the bus, the driver yelling *slow down* out the bus window. Dinner was on the table, dry pork chops and canned corn, brown-and-serve rolls that Mama must have baked too high since the tops were gooey and the bottoms burned. Daddy was already sitting at the head of the table like his rich uncle had finally got out of the poor house and gave him the kingdom.

After dinner we heard Mama sniffing and whimpering through the walls, crying and then screaming to Daddy. "Dinner was terrible," she said. "I'm thirty-two years old and all I'm getting out of life is a good meal." In a few days, days that let us get comfortable with her, let us stop thinking about her as a miracle, she was gone. We were all shocked. Daddy didn't come out of his room that first day at all. But nobody took it harder than Greg. I was a child too, ten years old, but even I could see Greg was hurting. For days, he looked for Mama. I'd catch him in the basement, in the far-off place near the creek where we burned our trash or waiting on at the edge of the yard, like he was going to be the first one to see her when she came down the road. Finally, one day I found him in a field a little ways down the road from the house, asleep in the tall, itchy grass.

"Come on, Greg. Let's go," I said and held out my hand, ready to lead him home.

"Is Mama back?" he said. I thought about what to tell him, a boy, a child of six. I could have said a hundred things to make it better. Start with love. Start with love. "She's never coming back. Never in your life."

"You remember that time Mama came? Remember?" And I started to cry fat ugly tears that wouldn't stop, tears I hadn't expected. "It was only for a few days, remember?" The women beside me looked

68

at me with pity, their conversation stopped, their words caught up in the air.

"Don't start that shit," Greg said, but his voice cracked. He remembered. "Don't even start it."

I wanted to hold on to Greg like somebody should have those many years ago. In the movies they put their spread fingers on either side of the glass, trying to get as close to touch as they could. Like that could ever be enough.

"Just tell Daddy to get me out," Greg said and motioned for the guard to take him away.

"What's Serena cooking tonight?" Shelia asks, her face looking all open and revealed like a topless sandwich. That's exactly what she looked like. A topless sandwich.

"I'm getting some dessert unless I'll miss something good," Shelia says. They all laugh. They were patient with her, no matter what she did.

"I'm getting some too," I say.

The dessert bar was across from the main warmers of food. A bakery/dessert bar they call it, but all they had baked were a few hard cookies and some yeast rolls at the most. A young black guy I didn't recognize was working the bakery box, surrounded by glass partitions so customers could see him knead the yeasty bread and take the trays of cookies out of the large ovens, like baking was a spectator sport. I glance at him for a second — enough to figure that he won't stop his work to take me in. He goes back to shifting the made cookies to the right stack, the blackened trays he places beside the ovens.

"You better watch that ice cream, girl," the man says to Shelia. "You know what happens," the man grins at Shelia, his eyes running the distance from her thighs to her face.

"Can't I have a little?" Shelia teases.

I wanted to tell her that everybody knows that Polo, her boyfriend, sees his old girl-friend when he's not with her. I wanted to tell her not to think she's so special.

Shelia starts to walk away from the ice cream bar.

"Come back and see me," the man calls to her, watching her swish away.

I am left with my ice cream and two white women, one middle aged and one younger, in front of me now, in line to load their bowls with candy toppings.

"The moon is eclipsing Pleiades tonight," the younger one says, her skin the color pink of her cotton-candy sweater. She raises her eyebrows to the other like this information is interesting. "I read it in the *Journal Patriot.*"

"I'm not much into reading the stars," the older woman smiles and stirs the aluminum bins like they are pots on a stove.

"Oh, I don't either. No horoscopes or anything like that. Goodness," the woman in the pink sweater chooses a spoon and stabs it into the gut of her mound of ice cream. "Anne says we need to get the birds together," she says.

"A play date? For birds?" The woman grins, her smile ugly as a keloid on her face. "That's a new one on me."

"Well, I guess it's a play date. I guess you could call it that," the first one laughs and then they both do. "I guess that's what it is."

"What kind of bird do you have?" I say before I realize I've said it.

"Excuse me," the older woman says, trying to remind me that I wasn't part of their conversation.

"A Quaker parrot and a budgie," the younger woman interrupts but concentrates on the M&Ms like getting them in her bowl is brain surgery.

The older woman glances at the younger one, a smirk in her eyes, like I'm not a 3-D

71

person who can see what she does, like it would take so much for her to show me the smallest kindness.

"Just move," I say too loud, the *move* a sorrow in my mouth. "I don't have all day."

The man behind the glass snorts, not bothering to shade his grin with his hand or look away. Both of the women look at me now. The younger one closes her mouth and walks away. The older one considers standing her ground, but gives up, leaving her ice cream on the counter like she was trying to prove she was there.

I don't bother with the toppings but take my plain vanilla scoop back to the table. None of them have paid any attention to me and for once, I'm glad. Shelia is talking and waving her spoon as she explains. Her ice cream forms a growing puddle in the plastic bowl. She is going to Tennessee to the mountains, to Pigeon Forge with Polo. They have a room and will be able to hear a creek, walk to a pancake house, travel in happiness along mountain roads in a rental car. They are looking forward, hoping, can't waiting. Everybody watches Shelia. They nod and chew, her story in harmony with what they want to know about life.

"If Polo's not with Jerica," I say, and the spell is broken. All eyes fix on me, and their faces say, this is all we expect.

"What are you trying to say," Shelia yells. "What, Dee? Say it."

I don't see any understanding in these faces that look so much like mine. They are waiting for me to pass over like a quick nasty rain. "Nothing, Shelia. I swear to God. I wasn't trying to say nothing." But it's too late. I grab my pocketbook to my shoulder, stand up, and walk away from the booth.

"Dee, what are you doing?" Mark says, but Daddy interrupts him.

"Let her go on," I hear Daddy say to my retreating back.

The air outside is cool but not unpleasant on my face and arms. Still, I don't want to be out in the open. I find my car on the side of the building, but I don't want to go home yet. I get in the cramped back seat, like a passenger. This feels stupid. It does. But I have to do something, and it is dusk now, the sunset over, but too early for screaming, too early to cry out like a fool. Too early to realize that nobody will stop for you while there is still light. Way too early to know for sure that nobody will listen, good enough or long enough to hear you yelling over and over: I am so afraid.

WE ARE TAKING ONLY WHAT WE NEED

In my father's house there were many dogs. Or at least the memory of dogs. Brown or garbage gray with slick short hair, fully grown things with generic faces, like a child's cartoon idea of Dog. We call them end-of-the-liners, last days-ers, apocalypse dogs. These dogs didn't bother to bond with us, but stuck out their paws, not to shake hands but so we could slit their wrists and get it the hell over with. All of them were mutts. Every last one. Nobody dropped his beloved purebred on our Carolina dirt road in the middle of the night.

There were puppies, not many, but a few curly haired sweet things with lying round faces that betrayed us every time they peed all over the rug or kept us up with their crying, their baying, their inconsolable whining for the loss of a body warm with the familiar stank of their own.

A few of them came to us intentionally

from the hands of desperate neighbors who couldn't stand to drown the whole litter if there was another way. But most were unlucky and landed on my daddy's land, as unplanned as his children, and just as one-shoulder-shrug tolerated. We are not cruel. We are country. We don't heart dogs. You aren't likely to see a black, country woman's dog in a Christmas sweater. We are not dog mommies. Nobody goes out of their way to get called bitch. We know that God intended dogs to live outside in the relative wild, by their cunning, instincts, and not by whatever faith they put in us. My people don't need reminding that God might love the sparrow but the dirty mutt fends for himself. Dogs might spend some sad days in search of cool or shelter under a sagging porch, but not in the house, not beside us on the sheets, not with their rough tongues on our faces; not in any communion that feels set apart — just us, just us. In my father's house, no dog got more love than a day.

For every known there is a mystery. In the summer of my eleventh year, my mother moved out of Daddy's house to an apartment across town with her best friend, Dot, and Dot's boyfriend. For some reason, my brother Cal and I were not surprised and accepted the change like we'd seen it coming. School was almost out for the summer vacation and for the first time in her life, my mother took a full-time job. Daddy had no choice but to hire a baby-sitter. I expected somebody I knew from church, maybe Tonette or Rhonda, bored half-children desperate for an opportunity to impart their just-won knowledge to a couple of younger kids. *In my class, two girls have already had babies. Yes, I have hair under my arms. Yes, I understand the world and all its mysteries. No, I was never, ever as pathetic as you.* But Daddy fooled us and brought in a stranger. A white stranger. A high-school girl, one of the children of the men he worked with at the shop, no older than Tonette or Rhonda, but infinitely more interesting.

It doesn't take much to intrigue a dirt-road child, and our new, white baby-sitter quickly became the subtext to all of our talks and speculations. Is her scalp white too? Her butt? What about her poop? Why aren't her knees darker than her legs?

Her name was Tammy and I couldn't make up my mind about her. My brother didn't like her face. "She looks mean," he said, but I didn't see mean as much as vexed, like a princess touring a barn. My mother choked a laugh. "That's your daddy," she'd said, like that explained everything. Tammy's hair was too short for my taste, a boy's do, and her favorite activity looked to be running her fingers in it, like she couldn't be sure from one minute to the next that it would still be attached. She wore her shorts too short, and her pale veiny thighs wobbled with the extra twenty or twenty-five pounds she carried below the belt. She was not beautiful. But she liked to laugh and, in unexpected moments, you could feel the weight of her need for you to like her. I was not accustomed to that need, especially from anyone older than me.

From the beginning of the arrangement, my grandmother did not approve. "Plenty of black children need a job," she'd said. "What's wrong with the Banner girl?" Her most surprising comment was an admonition: "Don't get near her when she's wet." My grandmother wrinkled her nose in disgust. "White people smell like wet dog."

The novelty of Tammy wore off quickly. She was just another baby-sitter doing as little as possible until it was time for Daddy to drive her home when his shift ended. But just when we had her figured out and settled in our thinking, she flipped the script on us and showed up at our house on a Saturday morning with Daddy. Cal and I were sitting on the floor in front of the television watching cartoons, eating cereal that we made ourselves. We thought our father was asleep until we heard his rumbling voice, along with peals of Tammy's silly laugh floating down the hall. "Is that Daddy?" I said. Cal shrugged and kept watching a Looney Tune.

"Look who's here," Daddy said.

"Hey, Portia," Tammy said in a fawning way that took me a minute to recognize was her being nice, much nicer than she ever was alone with us during the week.

"Are you going to work?" I said to Daddy, ignoring Tammy the best I could.

My father grinned, like he'd been caught in a lie. "No, Tammy is here to help me out today." My father glanced at Tammy and she loosed a giggle, both of them in on a joke I'd come on too late. "She's on her way to the flea market. Get ready and go with her."

I had never been to a flea market before. The one in Reidsville was held every week from Friday through Sunday at the county fairground, and though I knew it couldn't be so, I held out a wish that a flea market might be a fair, smelling of sawdust and spun sugar with vendors of a different sort, maybe, but still with flashing lights, bright games of chance with cheaply stuffed animals, and rides I loved that creaked with age and nobody-gives-a-damn neglect.

Our flea market was on a clay hill, and from the car, all I'd ever been able to see were hand-painted signs announcing hours and vegetables, used furniture, antiques, junk, something for everyone. "Can Cal come?"

"It will just be us girls." Tammy bent in my direction to better look me in the eye. Even from three feet away, her teenager's acne-pocked and sleep-lined face made me take a step back. "That'll be fun, don't you think?" she asked. I didn't like Tammy's sudden adult tone. I wished she would ignore me like she usually did so I could know what to do. "That's okay. I'll stay here," I said.

"Go get your shoes on," Daddy said in a voice I knew meant he was done talking. From inside the house, Tammy squealed at something Daddy said, like a child or a pig. How could I have ever liked either of them? If I'd been a different kind of child, I would have locked the door behind me.

The Reidsville flea market was no carnival. Rows of age-grayed wooden tables filled with what looked like junk: a toaster beside

Raggedy Ann, a set of plastic plates next to a funeral wreath still in the plastic, worn jeans someone's three-year-old had outlasted, toys and dolls long discarded. The whole place looked like the debris from a flood. And I thought of the junk from my own girlhood: baby dolls I held and diapered, or Barbies I made do unspeakable things to each other, the posters and T-shirts of the boy singers I loved, the plastic, backless, high-heeled shoes I coveted with an achy sickness until I finally owned their pink, glittery flamboyant puffiness of feathers — all that life came springing back at me when I looked at the table sagging with other people's memories.

Only the rookie salespeople, the people who thought it might be fun to take a weekend and make a few bucks, worked to make the sale. They had yet to learn that when everything was a rock-bottom, desperate price, you will buy or you won't — nobody can tell you different. But most of the vendors had the calm resignation of old hands or the damned. And in that last-hour-on-earth way, the sellers resembled the customers, the couples, the occasional lone man in coveralls, the older women with their daughters and grandchildren, all dressed in faded denim and comfortable cotton shirts, a found treasure or two in overused, mostly white plastic grocery bags hanging from their arms like icicles.

Tammy was comfortable in the group. She knew the rhythm of the crowd and could tell just when to push forward and take her place at a table. She knew to keep her hands in her pockets. Don't touch unless you've made a serious plan to take it home with you. Be coy. No sense in lingering if no item sparkled.

"I need to get to the Sock Man," she said and pointed to the end of the row. "He works with your daddy." She nodded in explanation.

The long warehouse that was Seagel furniture factory couldn't have been more of a secret to me if my father worked for the CIA. A few times, I saw him walk into the building or jog out, fine particulates of wood pulp spread across his skin like a rash.

Tammy and I stopped at the booth of a snaggletoothed man standing at the back of his sock-filled van, its saloon doors flung open. The man had socks everywhere: women's socks, knee socks, athletic socks, lace-topped socks for babies, Gold Toes for men, even socks that needed garters were flung over an empty box looking long and dangerous like black eels.

"Hey, Sock Man," Tammy said.

"Come here, girl." The man grabbed Tammy in a big hug, pressed his fingers into her soft back, his fingernails filthy moons. "You looking sweet, baby doll," he announced too loudly.

"What kind of deal you got for me?" Tammy teased as she turned her fat face up to Sock Man's leathery one, looking as wide-eyed and vulnerable as if she were his own beloved little girl.

"You get what you want, hear?" he said.

I wanted to be able to get what I wanted. To giggle into my hand while the world opened up.

Tammy found the box of socks she wanted. I watched her as best I could as I turned over one pair of socks then another, carefully, like I was afraid a lizard might slither from underneath. "You want some?" she said to me. I shook my head. I didn't have a dime, and I wouldn't spend money on socks if I did. Tammy picked out three pairs each with festive pom-poms on the back, Sock Man's most expensive kinds, but he wouldn't take more than a dollar for all three pairs.

"You enjoy them footies," he said, and winked at Tammy.

Tammy took her time at the next couple of tables. I wanted to go home. I wanted my mother.

"Tammy! Tam!" A young man yelled at us from behind. He caught up with us and flung his arms over Tammy's shoulders. "What are you doing here, loser?"

"Loser, hell," Tammy said and shrugged him off of her.

"Look here at this," he said and put on a pair of novelty glasses with big black rims and a plastic penis for a nose. "Dick glasses," he said, barely able to contain himself. " 'Spec-dick-acles!' You get it? They've got a whole box of them at Len's booth."

"Freak," Tammy said, but I could tell she was pleased.

I couldn't stand to watch Tammy flirt again and inched away from her and the high-energy boy to a colorful table a few feet away. What I thought from a distance were giant balloons stretched out and flattened turned out to be flags. Not American flags, but fun flags with picket fences, birdhouses, sleeping cats, kids'-art daisies and daffodils, or North Carolina State in blood red and white, the dandy wolf mascot smirking from the flag's center. I wanted to be the kind of person who flew a flag like this, owned one for each season. I wanted to touch the slick material to my face, feel thick threads of the decorations' top stitching on my fingertips, but I didn't dare. A white woman watched me from her perch on a folding lawn chair, the old-fashioned kind with wide nylon strips woven like a basket for the top and seat. She hadn't spoken to me, and there was no sign that she found me in the least adorable.

I was about to walk away when an iron bank with the beveled edges of a coffin caught my attention. On the top of the coffin was the coal-black face of a man, soup-cooling lips red and split wide open like a gash, his hands in corpse pose over his chest, grinning even in death. I'd seen mammies before: turn her over and salt comes rushing from her head; open her handles to let her squeeze your ground beef into patties; she is a teapot, a drip spoon; use her any way you want and she is still working, still just as hilarious. But I'd never seen a coffin. I backed away from the table. I wanted my mother. The woman got up from her chair and began to arrange her merchandise, though I had touched nothing. I wanted my mother.

"Where did you get to?" Tammy said, forgetting to be nice.

"Nowhere. Can we go?"

The woman looked at Tammy then back at me, trying to figure out our relationship. Tammy sucked her lips and glared at the woman until the woman's wrinkled face was forced to turn away from us. "Come see what I found."

Tammy held my forearm, pulled me gently with her around the corner of the building. A young woman with big curls sat on a small towel beside a cardboard box full of puppies. Three of them scampered over one another, tearing at the side of the box, their nails sounding like a rake against the cardboard.

"Go ahead and look at them," the woman said. "They're pure breeds. I wish I could keep every last one of them, but I got more than I can handle as it is."

"What kind are they?" I asked.

"What kind? The daddy is a German shepherd. He's been trained good by my husband. If you know anything about a shepherd, you know they are some smart dogs. The mama is a chow chow. See, you can tell here by the tongue." The woman reached into the box and pulled out the least-excited pup, stuck her finger into his mouth to show his black tongue. "That's how you can tell," she said. I held out my arms to hold the tamest of the puppies. I'd never had a pet at all, unless you count the dyed-pink baby chick I had for a day. I had marveled at the soft Easter bird, twitching from fear in the palm of my hand, until it squatted, alive, not a doll at all, and green, runny poop oozed on my hand and I flicked the bird to the ground.

The puppy stayed calm as I stroked his fur and held him to my chest to feel his heart beating faster than I would have thought possible for such a tiny creature. He turned his flat face to look at me without interest or concern. I was told to love my brother, though I couldn't yet see why, so I tolerated him, which seemed more than fair. My parents knew I loved them, though what part of that feeling was need I couldn't say. But this little dirt-smelling dog, I knew I loved.

"Will Daddy let us have one of them?" I whispered. I needed Tammy as an ally in this venture, otherwise I wouldn't have a chance. Tammy laughed, tucked a puppy under each of her arms. "We're taking them all."

■ ■ ■ ■

Tammy turned in the driver's seat and said, "No shitting in the car," to the puppies, who stopped wriggling long enough to listen to her. Neither of us admitted it, but we were nervous on that ride home. Neither of us had any idea what Daddy might say.

"We got something," Tammy announced as she hopped out of the car. Daddy got up from his position in the lounge chair on the carport and slowly made his way to the car, suspicion halting his walk.

"What the hell?" Daddy opened the back door and glared at the box. "What are you thinking?"

"I'm thinking that we can all have one. The kids and you and me. How about that?" Tammy leaned against my father, playfully bumping him with her hip. "They're pure breeds."

"Pure breeds, hell. Look how little they are? They're too young." Daddy sighed. "They ain't even weaned yet."

Tammy and I looked at our dogs. They were small, but aren't all puppies small? How were we to know they weren't weaned?

"The woman said she already sold four of them. These are the only three left."

"Sold hell. She might have got another fool to take them dogs, but she ain't sold nothing."

"Why do you have to ruin everything?" Tammy yelled. I wasn't used to anyone talking back to my father. I wasn't sure what to expect. "Why is everything a problem with you?"

To my shock, my father looked like an embarrassed boy scolded in front of his friends. I almost felt sorry for him. "You like them?" Daddy said to me.

I loved one of them, but I wasn't sure at all how I felt about them all. They were clearly unruly. Three dogs, with all their sharp teeth and nails, nasty habits I knew without anybody telling me, wouldn't be fun to police. "Yeah, I like them," I said, trying not to look in Tammy's direction. She had nearly done the impossible, and the last thing I wanted was to ruin it all by making us look like co-conspirators.

"Okay, then." Daddy lifted the box out of the car. Tammy peered into the box, stopped Daddy before he could get the pups to the yard.

"Look at him," she said, pointing to one of the dogs. "Look at his little face."

"Cal! Cal!" I yelled toward the house not willing to move or to take my eyes off of

Daddy for fear he might change his mind.

"We ought to throw this box of mutts in a creek," he said, trying to tease.

"Why would you say that? That's cruel."

Daddy shrugged, embarrassed again that his attempt at reconciliation backfired. "I wouldn't. That's just the way people used to do it. Either that, or leave them on the side of the road. People leave horses now. You know it?"

Tammy pursed her lips in disbelief. "No, they don't."

"They do. It takes a lot to feed a horse and ain't nobody got money to buy it. This guy at the shop ended up with two like that. Went outside to his pasture and instead of two horses, he had four." Daddy laughed. "They don't work that damn fast."

Tammy didn't seem sure that she wasn't being put-on, and she smacked Daddy's arm to signal that he was back in her good graces. "You think you can tell me anything and I'll believe it."

I knew Daddy wasn't joking. I could tell he was serious, and the idea of waking up in the morning to the baleful, ignorant eyes of a horse terrified me. I concentrated on the box of puppies as Daddy settled it onto the ground. The pups tried to get out of the box, huffing and puffing, standing on, and crawling over, one another for advantage.

"Cal, get out here," Daddy yelled.

"What?"

"You come out here and see what."

Daddy was not the kind of parent to play one child against the other. There was no good child or bad child at our house. Only the certainty that at any moment you could go wrong and open the wounds of his anger, make the mistake that taxed or burdened him, told the story with your exasperated sigh, your briefly rolled eyes, the whined *why not* or *everybody else can* whetting your lips, but you dared not say it, since the subtext meant that you never had appreciated his sacrifices and never would.

Cal stopped at the door and saw the box thumping from inside with fuzzy life, his face a picture of joy I can't recall to this day without tears. Cal reached in the box to touch a pup, though none of them stopped the struggle to escape.

For an hour, an evening, I'm not sure, since everything had changed for us, Cal and I sat with the puppies and watched them. To our delight, their combined weight finally succeeded in turning the box over onto the grass. All three puppies, from instinct, from first sight, from the animal knowledge that danger was close, too close, ran out of our yard as fast as they could, but of course we caught them.

The puppies were too young and cried all night. Before we fell asleep, we heard them whimper at the dark, after we must have closed our eyes and forgotten them, and their whines settled like fine sand in our ears and nostrils. They had one another, but that wasn't enough. At some time in the night, Daddy covered them with a trash can to try to muffle the pitiful sound. We didn't know they weren't weaned. How could we have known?

The quiet one, my puppy, died in two days. I startled awake as I always did and went straight outside to see her. I hadn't even had a chance to decide on a name, though Iggy, Otch, Scamp, and Victoria were all in the running. I'd never named a living thing and wanted it to be just right.

While the other puppies were already out of the box, my pup appeared to sleep. While her brother and sister sniffed at gravel or dug their baby paws in the red clay, looking for a nugget of something killed, a disgusting treat under every piece of detritus, every stray piece of litter, my dog stayed put in the box. As he did every weekday, Daddy had gone to pick up Tammy to baby-sit.

"Daddy, she won't get out."

"Let the dog sleep."

"No, she's not. She's not asleep."

"You touched a dead dog?"

I shook my head. "I didn't."

"Don't touch it again."

"I didn't, Daddy," I said. I knew better. My mother was a champion napper, a log, until sometimes Cal and I, hovering over her, whispered to each other, wanting to poke her gently, rest our hands on her chest, to feel the rise and fall of her breath. *Mama? Mama?* But we didn't dare touch her. We would know what we most feared. If we were alone in the world and nothing would ever stand between us and the dark, at least we would not touch that sadness for ourselves. Ma wouldn't wake until whatever it was reached in and shook her upright. The explanation like most answers was a simple one. Our mother's nights were full of vacuuming, laundry, staring out a dirty window at nothing at all, but not with sleep. All Cal and I knew of our mother's nightlife was a wafer of yellow light under the door, the lulling factory sound of a sewing machine in our shared dreams.

"She didn't know he was dead, Roger," Tammy said, startling me by calling my father by his name. I had forgotten that he had one.

Daddy shook the box, kicked it, mumbled under his breath something that sounded like it had teeth. He came from around the house with a shovel and dragged it behind him, along with the box, to the woods. He would bury my dog, I thought. Daddy was back in a minute, maybe less, the sides of the empty box bent, torn, and scratched, banged against his leg. In the long afternoon, when I could take no more television and the sweltering heat of the house or my brother's hundred slow-motion trips to stand, door open, and examine the insides of the mostly empty refrigerator, I went to bury my puppy myself. I wasn't far in the woods when I saw her on her side, arms and legs pointed straight out like a toy. I started to dig a hole with a stick, when her rigid death, immutable and undignified, stung me. Many years later, I would tell the story of my puppy, my first pet, and how I labored with that stick, dug the terrible hole, patted the earth into a mound on top of her the way it is done, made a monument to her with sticks and rocks, instead of leaving her like trash.

"You got other dogs," Daddy said, which I knew meant that he was sorry.

■ ■ ■ ■

Right before lunch, the white boy from the flea market came to our house. I hadn't noticed when he arrived, but there he was in our kitchen, hanging on Tammy like a monkey.

The boy had his hands around her waist from behind, looking directly at me in the doorway.

"Stop. She's going to see," Tammy whispered.

"She don't care. Do you?" The boy nuzzled Tammy's neck, not waiting for my reply.

"Go," Tammy said shrugging him off. "I'll see you later." The boy walked past me to his low-riding car. Tammy glanced a look of worry at me. "Tomorrow we can make snow-cones. I know how. You want to?"

"Yeah," I said. The lie was such a good one even Tammy believed it.

"Don't tell your daddy, okay?"

I nodded, though I couldn't be sure what I'd do.

In the weeks following, Mike came to our house nearly every day, sometimes with McDonald's french fries, sometimes with candy bars so melted we had to lick most of the chocolate off the wrappers. There was still no reason to like him.

Cal's dog, Brownie, lived for nearly three weeks after mine. And then, just like my dog's, his death was quiet and sudden, except this time when we woke, Daddy had already come back from the woods, had already put the shovel back to the shed in the backyard. Bobo, Tammy's dog, was the only pup left. In the strange logic that sometimes afflicts animals and children, Bobo ignored the children, tolerated Tammy, but loved my father, the person in the house who paid her the least attention. Bobo followed Daddy around the house, to the basement, rested beside him as he worked on refinishing his furniture, perked her ears, the insides unexpectedly pink like a turned-down lip, when she heard Daddy's tires hit the gravel at the top of the road. Bobo insisted that Daddy love her, made sure that if any of his love happened to fall like crumbs from a table, she would be there to catch it on her tongue.

Daddy did not seem to mind. In fact, Bobo had privileges given to no other dog, and, only a few times, to children in Daddy's house. Bobo got to come into Daddy's bedroom. I didn't know that for sure until I saw her for myself, chewing like a maniac on one of Tammy's flip-flops. The sight of the smelly dog on his carpet shocked me. That the world could be so different from what I imagined. That I could have been so wrong. Daddy and Tammy on his bed, Tammy leaned against the wobbling headboard like a starlet, while Daddy draped sideways at the foot of the bed, the bottoms of Tammy's blackened bare feet inches from Daddy's face. I saw him grab her calf. I saw her lean to him, her small breasts struggling to escape the lax policing of her tank top. Tammy was the first to notice me in the doorway.

"Your daughter is in here."

Daddy leapt up from the bed, scaring Bobo into stillness. "You ready to go home?" he said to Tammy.

Tammy laughed like Daddy had just said something hilarious. "I'm ready, honey," she giggled.

It was dark already and Daddy had still not returned from dropping Tammy off at her home. Cal was too impatient to wait any longer for dinner, so he ate a row of saltines from the box, three slices of American cheese, the cellophane wrappers floating behind him down the hall as he chewed, the last of the family-sized box of Lucky Charms cereal sprinkled like gold dust in his hands. When the phone rang, I was sure it was Daddy, but Tammy's voice, younger than in person, sang over the line. "Portia, are you okay?"

"Yeah," I said. "Daddy's not here."

"Portia, I've got to tell you something."

"Where's Daddy?"

"I don't know. Isn't he there?"

I nodded no, though, of course, she couldn't see my response.

"I have to tell you something important." Tammy sighed like what she was about to say might hurt her. I didn't want to hear it.

"I was pregnant. You know what I mean? The baby died, but I was still pregnant. You know?"

I was eleven. I didn't know. I had no idea.

"Are you surprised?"

"Yes," I said, though the fact made no impression on me. Nothing of what she said had shape or existence for me. I was years from understanding the consequences.

"You want to know what it felt like?"

I am eleven years old. I am eleven years old. "Yeah," I said aware that I had whispered.

"Nothing else in the world. I swear, just wait. I knew I was but didn't tell anybody. I got tests, three of them. They were all positive, but I already knew it. A couple of weeks later I started bleeding." Tammy sniffled into the phone. She was crying. "Something comes sliding down my leg. Like Jell-O, like grape Jell-O."

"Why?" I asked.

"It was a baby," Tammy's voice became hard as she tried to get me to understand. "Your sister." Tammy wailed.

I waited while Tammy sniffled into the phone.

"You know what I did," she whispered like she couldn't tell any bigger secret. "I ate some of it," Tammy whispered. "I really did," she insisted like I'd protested.

"What did it taste like?"

Tammy was so quiet on the phone for so long I thought, for a moment, she'd hung up. Apparently, I'd asked just the right question to convince her that she would get nothing useful from me.

"I don't know. Nothing. I just wanted you to know. Your daddy's not gonna tell you, but you should know."

By the time Daddy got home, the country sky had turned scary dark, the kind that came and dissolved before your eyes. Daddy plopped himself at the kitchen table, rested his head in his hands.

"Portia, sit down here." Daddy scraped a

chair across the wood floor in my direction.

"You doing all right?"

In my life, I couldn't remember a day that my father had asked how I was. He was Old School, and Old School parents don't ask about your welfare. If you are fed and not bleeding, you are fine. You learn to believe this. There is no secret part of you that is not cured by food or a tourniquet. If you suspect differently, tamp it down, the feeling will go away.

"You can tell me the truth," he said.

"Okay."

"Has Mike been to this house?"

I must have looked confused.

"Did Tammy ever bring anybody to this house? Anybody? Tell your daddy the truth."

Daddy's softness wounded me. He wanted me to break his heart. I didn't know it then, but the question that breaks your heart never wants an answer. That question is looking for a miracle and just the right combination of words to make the sharp pieces of the world dull and harmless, floating by like flakes in a snow globe.

"This boy came. A white one," I said, feeling the power of the knowledge, oblivious to my father's pain. "He came a lot."

Daddy's face collapsed.

"Was that Mike?" I asked, feeling small

and young again. The temporary power from hurting dissipated, leaving my chest concave and desperate for air.

Daddy didn't answer.

"Go on in the living room and watch TV."

Daddy got on the phone in the kitchen, and in minutes, he was crying into the receiver. He didn't care one damn bit if she didn't love him. Oh, so he was funny, was that it? He was not the dramatic one. He was not an old man. He'd show her old man. She was the one better look out for the police. He had a fucking life!

After he slammed down the phone, Daddy locked himself in his room, came out fully composed with his shotgun in his hand.

"Where are you going?"

"Stay in here."

"Where are you going?"

Here's what I don't know. If Daddy called Bobo, I did not hear it. Maybe the puppy bounded up to him as usual. But I suspect that small lives learn to be shrewd. Though Bobo had never seen a shotgun, and the pup had no need to fear the object or the man, the dog surely smelled the stench of a rotting place in my father, the awful wound that made him the worst combination of desperate and determined. But Bobo probably waited, too knowing, too forgiving, to run. I heard the squeal of the pup so close to the shotgun blast I couldn't swear they didn't happen at the same time.

I ran to the door in time to see my father pick up the dog and carry it to the back seat of the car. My father's shirt was stained like he'd been the one shot. Blood marked his middle like a fatal wound.

"Daddy!" I screamed, though I knew what I was seeing couldn't be true.

"Get Cal and let's go," he said.

I ran back inside and pulled up Cal from the couch, dragged him by the arm as I wiped my eyes. "Just come on," I hissed.

"In the front," Daddy said. "And don't look back there."

But I looked, I couldn't help it, and all I saw was a sleeping dog, and in that light, the only evidence of hurt was a patch of blood-stuck fur on her tiny back.

Daddy said nothing until we got to Mama's apartment.

"Go on. Get on out."

Cal climbed out obediently while I sat waiting for something to come to me to say. "I hate you," I said with calm surprise, like I'd just discovered it.

"I know it," he said, and drove away while we stood like orphans on the sidewalk.

■ ■ ■ ■

We heard that Daddy left that dead dog on Tammy's parents' doorstep. He parked his car down the road from their house until the police made him move. They say he called her so many times that her daddy yanked the phone down from the kitchen wall, breaking it into pieces. My mother said he was crazy. "He loves you until he has to work for it," she said. "Then he's an ass."

But Daddy had it right. If I learned nothing else, I learned that love demands tribute. And whatever else you can say about crazy love, it is tenacious, it must be hyperbolic to survive or cooler heads, wise people with good sense — practical sorts who never find themselves drunk, crying, and stupid in the middle of the road — all those people and their boring practical reasonableness and their this-is-the-best-way, they win. And if that happens, love never gets the chance to look you in the eyes, inches from your face, never gets to say, *Let me, let me, let me. You won't regret it. Let me.* Oh, Daddy, forgive me. I have been a fool.

Unassigned Territory

Leslie Pawlowski parks her blue Horizon on the shoulder of the dirt road — the best shade we can find. July is a killer in North Carolina. It's always hot as blazes, hot enough for you, hot enough to fry eggs and on and on. We are in the thick of it, mid-morning, our dresses clinging to our backs, way far in the middle of nowhere, preaching door to door, working in our congregation's unassigned territory. This is the kind of dirt road, *Hee-Haw,* overalls, straw-in-the-teeth place even we Southerners make fun of. Pikes and Wagoners country. Did you hear the one about the Pike girl who went to a town doctor? The doctor says to her mother, 'Ma'am has this girl had intercourse?' and the mother, hands wringing, says, 'I don't rightly know, doctor, but if she needs it, you make sure you give it to her.'

The passenger's side window sticks in the middle of going up or down. Piece of junk car. And on the way to every door, we shed bits of poly foam from the car's cracked upholstery. Leslie has a great attitude about her poverty. "Halcyon, salad days" she will remember with a withering chuckle when her future kids complain of their own first cars. We've visited too many houses without updating our field-service records, and we stop before we forget the details. We need to keep records. Records for ourselves, for the congregation file on the territory, and for the official log we store at the Kingdom Hall.

"What was that woman's name at the blue trailer, Steph?"

I shuffle through my notebooks knowing I won't find any useful information. You are supposed to write things like *Ruth Boaz, 123 Main Street, blue trailer, lived in town all her life, no husband in the house, four kids — one still at home. Took the July 1989 Awake, "Making the Most of Your Youth." Expressed an interest in tarot. Bring magazine* Why Godly People Shun Spiritism. My records are to say the least incomplete. I wrote: *Trailer is a nightmare.* Looks like the time my brother and I played drug czar with an old suitcase and Monopoly money. Ryan threw my clothes and shoes out of the dresser and closet screaming, "Where's the real stash!

Where's the real stash!"

I'm praying that Leslie won't ask to see what I've written. I've been at this long enough that I don't need any guidance from my field-service partner. Sometimes Leslie will say things like, "you're writing a book over there, aren't you," but she never pries.

"Shoot. I hate to leave her name off. She was nice, too," Leslie sighs.

Nice to Leslie means that she didn't cuss us, that she didn't shoo us away or hide behind her curtains, her hand over the mouth of her child like a kidnapper. "But Mama," the kid would manage through her fingers, "there's some girls on the porch." "Shh," I imagine her saying, "Do you want to be saved? Is that what you want?"

This lady had stood on her rickety porch — sullen and quiet, her eyes never leaving my brown face. Leslie, even with her Minnesota accent, was apparently okay. Brown woman on the porch trumps Yankee invader any day. To be fair, they don't get too many black Jehovah's Witnesses out here. There are only two black Jehovah's Witness families in town, for a total of six people. Besides, although our congregation got to every door in the city limit at least three times a year, the unassigned territory, this deliverance of woods, creeks, and black snakes, gets worked only once a year if we were lucky. More likely, these people won't see any of us for eighteen to twenty-four months. Imagine the odds of seeing a black Jehovah's Witness in the territory. That's lotto odds.

Besides seeing no black people, there are four important things to remember about the unassigned territory:

1) You are as remote as you can get in this new world. Way out in the boonies, mostly white Southerners who've been holed up here for generations, living on winding dirt roads that lead to more winding dirt roads, with houses, the occasional mansion, trailers, and shacks out of sight from each other. They like it that way. 2) Everybody and his dog has a dog. At least one loose, ugly mutt with cockleburs in his unloved fur and filled with the kind of hatred that only comes from at last finding a body more miserable than yourself. 3) Apparently the trauma of a visit from Jehovah's Witnesses is so great that just the glimpse of your *Watchtower* will act as a Proustian mnemonic causing the householder to wax nostalgic about your last visit. Never mind that someone from your or any congregation left a tract in the door two years ago. You will hear over and over, "Some of ya'll was just here." 4) There

is nothing good about the unassigned territory.

Leslie explained the "Offer for the
Month," trying to regain the householder's
attention. "This is our new book, *Enjoy Life
Forever on a Paradise Earth.*" Leslie dangled
the bright red cover at the woman. Even the
color pictures of laughing children and
fluffy sheep nuzzling up to male lions didn't
move the woman's eyes. She only had eyes
for me.

Does the missus want I should jig, a little
tap dance fuh yo pleasure, I wanted to ask,
but instead put on my best, "yes, I'm black,
but doggonit, not that black" face.

"You got that same Bible?" the woman
said to me.

"Yes ma'am." I held out my cardboard
covered *New World Translation* for her to
see. When I got baptized, I'd get a leather
one.

"That's plenty," she said, folding her arms
across her chest. "I know the Bible when I
see it."

Leslie gave the woman an older *Watchtower* magazine that she wouldn't have to
request a donation for. Good move, Leslie.
She can get the literature into the house
and not risk rejection. Who knows? This
woman might even read it. She might

change her life around and be side by side with us in this very territory next year. You never know. That's why Leslie is a pro. She thinks about these kinds of things. I've seen her talk to grief-stricken and depressed people, whip out the Bible she seems to know by heart and without a blink show them that God is a fortress, a rock, a high place, a God of comfort, love, and forgiveness. And for a few seconds, I think she really lightens those people. It is no small thing to give a person even a moment of hope. Of course, when we go back the next week to follow up, those very same people slam their doors, order us away, looking like they could kill us. "Don't you tell me God loves me. Don't you dare."

Leslie is grooming me, though she doesn't think that I know. I have a big decision to make next year. To serve Jehovah during my youth (which is, by the way, the surprising twist ending to our magazine, *Making the Most of Your Youth*) or to go to college. I know that my congregation elders have told Leslie to help me do the right thing.

On the way past the car, past the tired old dog, through the patchy yard, I can't be sure, but I think I heard the woman say *wetback*. I don't know, it could have been the bigoted cicadas or heatstroke, but I think she called me a wetback. I wanted to put my finger in her crumpled face, her skin like the film from Krazy Glue and say something wise and cutting like, "Get your racial epithets right, Ms. Einstein." But fighting in the field service is looked down on. Truth be told, at 97 degrees and counting, Unnamed Householder had the virtue of being accurate. Not nice, but accurate. Besides, the sentiment for the Mexicans who were coming into the county taking all the glory jobs like picking apples for fourteen hours a day for less than minimum wage and apparently preaching door to door in glamour locales like Miller's Creek was enough to make anybody sick with envy. I wanted to tell Leslie what I thought I'd heard, but she was the sort of white person who refused to acknowledge racism. Just deny it and it won't exist. She'd say, "Well, I'm sure she didn't mean anything. Maybe she was concerned about the heat."

"What about the man on the tractor? Where did he say he lived?" Leslie asks. "I knew we should have stopped right then."

"Oh yeah," I say, stalling, shuffling through the pages.

My record:

Dear Martin Luther King: Sir, is this the

dream you meant? Me and this sweet girl from Minnesota in a steaming car? I met a black man weeks ago who was courting a pretty woman he thought would be his wife. But that Memphis day in early April, slow dragging in a school cafeteria at a dance, the music dropped like the piano player's final clink when the black hats show up and a man ran in screaming that you were gone. My new friend looked in the pretty woman's face, at the despair he wore himself and knew he could never see her again. I am hot today, but trying to remember you at 1400 High Rock Road.

"1400 High Rock Road," I say.

"Okay, you are good for something," Leslie grins, acting like a mother. She's only six years older than I am, but preaching is her career. Her family moved to North Carolina only three years ago to serve "where the need was greater," but Leslie is easily one of the most popular people there. She's a good girl, with a sweet disposition, and she has committed herself to the fieldwork. Leslie is a pioneer — out in service at least sixty hours a month every month. Sixty hours of door slammings, I-have-my-own-religions, I-was-just-on-my-way-outs, and lonely old women who will even talk about Jehovah to hear another voice in the room.

"Okay," Leslie says, handing me a Shasta

soda from her cooler; she always gets the cheap drinks. "Let's do two more houses. One if it's too far, okay?"

Thank God, thank God. Thank you. Thank you Dr. King, thank you. Thank you. "Are you sure? I'm up for another hour or so," I say, willing the bouncing hope in my chest to stay still for a few minutes, she might change her mind. "I mean, if you need the time. I'm up for it," I manage to say with almost a smile in my voice.

"I'll just have to make it up next week," Leslie says breezily. But I know that this month will be especially hard for her. She has all those hours to complete in these backwoods. Think about it. You can't just preach any old time. You have to come knocking at decent hours, after nine in the morning and before eight at night and preferably not during the dinner hour. You can only count the time you actually preach. That means the forty-five-minute drive out there — gratis. The ride in between these houses in the territory — if it is more than ten minutes, you eat it. The fifteen-minute lunch break is on your time, sister-friend. All to say that Jehovah's Witnesses need a union.

Leslie dribbles soda all over the bodice of her dress. No loss, as far as I'm concerned.

Leslie shops at Granny's Rejects or Let's Repel Men or some store like it. I couldn't believe the kinds of things this young woman puts on her body: shifts (really!), baggy sweaters, long full skirts, big prints that make muumuus blush like demure schoolgirls. These things the wardrobe for Leslie's plump, pink frame. A style my daddy dubbed, "to' up from the flo' up." Leslie has mostly given up on men. I knew that the secret wish of her heart was that Bruce Springsteen come into the Truth, but she was only hoping in her heart, not in her head. Lately, I've noticed her saying strange things like, "when I was young," or "if I were your age," or "that's for the kids." She is twenty-four. Though truth be told, she is getting a bit long in the tooth for a Jehovah's Witness bride. The faithful marry young rather than burn with desire (see the Pauline letters) and marry fast to get the pick of the litter of endangered young male believers. The congregation has already picked out my husband for me. A nice-looking white boy with a flounce of blond hair, unswiveling hips, and clunky clod-buster shoes. Bobby Ratliff. I like Bobby, don't misunderstand me, but only twelve-year-old virgins look at a dopey sixteen-year-old and think *what great marriage mate-*

rial. Lord knows that by rejecting Bobby I was dooming myself to Lesliedom. There was precious little else to choose from, few kids my age to even compare and contrast. Jim, another teenager in the congregation, is a possibility, but he and his sister Lisa are bad. Really bad. Once they brought a dirty magazine on the school bus, passed it around like a cold to the other kids. I noticed when it came to Bobby's seat, he wouldn't even look at the filthy cover, wouldn't even touch it. The worst, the absolute limit was when Jim and Lisa brought a Prince song for us to listen to. When Prince said *Controversy* (and he said it often) Jim and Lisa led the bus in the rollicking mispronunciation at the tops of their heathen lungs. A variation I'm sure the pre–Jehovah's Witness Prince would have V8-smacked his yellow forehead, if he'd heard, *Why didn't I think of that?* on his lips. Bobby and I didn't tell on Jim and Lisa, though we were tempted. We did explain (at every opportunity) to the other kids that though Jim and Lisa attended the Kingdom Hall, they weren't really of our sort. We insisted that we are the real Jehovah's Witnesses. Sure Jim and Lisa were clever and cool and fun, but *salvation?* I don't think so.

Lingering in a parked car in someone's

driveway is a definite no-no, an unwritten rule; you can't look like you're casing the joint. But we are in a little bit of slow motion today, staring ahead at the almost graveled road, the high weeds and bushes now covered with a thick layer of red dust. There has been no rain for days. We couldn't see the house that the record told us was straight ahead. Somehow this seemed important to me. If I had the words, I would say to Leslie, isn't it funny that we can't see the next house? Doesn't that mean something? I wanted to tell her that, to take her deeper into my head. I wanted her to understand me. Leslie wouldn't get it. She would admonish me to pray for guidance and direction and she'd be right. I know she'd be right. What was the alternative really? The house record warns us of one place at the edge of the territory to avoid. "NOT INTERESTED. GUN." I can't help but think that the gun fact should come first. We would have to come back when we were sure that Jim Caudle — gun wielder — had moved or died. Today we wouldn't even check.

"Your door," Leslie says. "You can have the last door of the day."

The house is sweet, small with a red tin roof. Someone must love the sound of the rain. Hippies probably. The gravel driveway looks fairly new, and sure enough, there was no record of the house in our files.

Wait for the dog. Some come on strong, yelping and moaning like they've been stranded on Jupiter with a host of unheralded moons. Others yap a quick impotent sound that came when you least expected it, their only surprise attack.

Nothing. Just the pleasant walkway of paver stones, dotted along the path to the door without any discernable pattern, terracotta pots full of red geraniums. I like this place. I like the porch and bent-wood furniture, the chunky table in the center with a five-year-old, a toddler on the potty. Another instance when pervs and parents have the same taste in art. But there was nothing pervy about this place. Just solid and permanent.

"Hello," I say to the outline of the woman's face behind the screen door.

"Yes," she says. Her accent says above the Mason-Dixon.

"Good morning," I say. "We are sharing a word from the Bible with our neighbors this morning."

"Your neighbors," the woman says, opening her screen door.

"Yes, ma'am," I smile. Stupid. Stupid.

Leslie would never have used a canned line like that.

"You've got a generous idea of neighbors," the woman grins.

"We've been going for a few hours now," I say, not sure of what I'm getting at.

"You must be hot then, let me get you some drinks," the woman starts back into her house. When my mother was a teenager she ironed clothes for Mrs. Rowe, an old white woman in town. When the black man who tended the yard needed a drink of water, Mrs. Rowe would grab the glass from under the sink, bring the water or tea out to him herself. When he was done, she'd rinse the glass out with Clorox water; store it back to its place. Something told me that this woman will not scurry to her kitchen for the Colored glass. Something told me she was for real.

"Oh, no ma'am," I begin. "We are ready to go home. You are actually our last stop today." Why did I say that?

"You are Jehovah's Witnesses, then?"

She got the name right. The number of people who just can't manage the name is astounding. We are the Jehovahs or simply Jehovah or worse the jokes: *Are you a Jehovah's Witness?* they ask. *No kidding, well, where's the accident?*

116

"I knew some Witnesses a few years back. I worked with one. Nice people. I admire the work you do."

"Thank you," I say.

"I've studied a number of faiths, as a lay person, I mean. The spiritual life is important."

I was right, she is a hippie.

"Well, we want everyone to hear the good news," Leslie chimes in, saving me. I'm blowing this call. "We are always happy to find people of faith in these times. You know that the perilous conditions that we live in have been predicted in scripture," Leslie pulls out her Bible. Some householders recoil, like you've just pulled a gun. *Okay, okay, put the Bible down. You don't want to do anything crazy.*

"Well, I'm not much for organized religion, but I do try to keep an open mind. I'm glad that God is available to everyone. Are you sure you don't want a drink? It is brutal out here."

"No," I say too vehemently. "But I'm Stephanie, nice to meet you."

"Well take this then," the woman pulls out a couple of bills from her jeans' pocket. "I'm Phyllis; I'd like to give you a donation for your work."

"Thank you," Leslie hands the woman

117

some new magazines, taking only one of the dollars from her open hand.

"Okay, so that was Phyllis, new magazines," Leslie writes in her record. "I'm giving you credit for placing those. We'll come back to see her next week." Leslie pretends to be having trouble thinking about what to write in the record, but I know she's trying to figure the best way to make this last call a teaching moment. "Listen, Steph, don't worry if you forget your sermon. I've done it. We all have. As hot as it is I can hardly remember my name. Anyways, you got a magazine placement. That's the important thing. I don't see much working out with Phyllis," Leslie screws her face into a conclusion. "She's fine, nice really, but we're not going anywhere with her." Leslie pauses, trying to find the most encouraging angle. "Of course, Jehovah is the judge, but she seemed to me too comfortable. I don't think we're going anywhere. If you don't stand for something, you'll fall for anything, right?"

But I am hardly listening. All I can think about is I am in love with Phyllis. It is too easy to point to her middle-class manners, the slick magazines with no celebrities on the covers, the coasters on the willow furniture, her kindness at the end of a long hot day. I wanted her. Wouldn't it be great to walk up to someone's house and just say, I am here and I want to be your friend? Kids do it all the time. No misunderstandings. None of that rooting around for larger meaning. Like with God. He has the key, right? He holds the keys to happiness and to life. Why can't we just show up at the door, just ask for them? Why can't I open a door, any door, and He be on the other side with a whole host of Phyllises saying, "Here you go. Enjoy." Even before this. Before being a Jehovah's Witness, I'd been a member of my grandmother's African Methodist Episcopal Church. Another world of dogged believers. Mama Jean preached on lonely dirt roads, in black neighborhoods, none of this white man's religion. Black places like Warrior Creek, Freedman, and Dula town. "Do you need to make water?" she'd warn before the services. Because there would be no possibility once we commenced. Remember, no hair-fooling, no gum, no candy, no giggling, no turning to look at the opening door, no smiling, no eye darting, no talking, no tapping of feet or fingers, clapping at up-tempo songs only, but not too vigorously like I've had no home training, no syncopation with the claps — leave that to the elders. No staring at anyone, even the spirit-filled or pitiable. And these are the easy rules, the ones for the very young. *No problem. No problem,* I say with nods. And if you are very good, do it all to your utmost like Noah, just so, you, too, will be rewarded with belief. Oh, Phyllis, to believe anyway. What are you made of? I start my house-to-house record:

Dear Philip Larkin: I have felt your breath on my heart today. Phyllis said she likes to keep an open mind and I fear this is the beginning. I will not go down the long slide with you, but stay safe, a dirtroader myself. It is safe here. The copse of pines, poplars and weeds years too far gone for bush hogging choke out everything but light. Don't you see that? If you can't, I can't love you. Doesn't scripture say to stay away from bad associates? Friends who will see you dead, all in the name of opening your mind? What about knowing every single thing for sure? What about that?

"A good day. Really good day," Leslie says. "How did you like your first visit to the territory? Different, huh?"

I nod.

"You seem preoccupied. Are you thinking about a certain young man?" Leslie starts the engine, grins at my shock that she takes for proof of her suspicion. My body shudders at the thought. I would see Bobby at the Kingdom Hall when Leslie drops me off. I'll see him the next morning at the Sunday service and the day after that on the bus. But the thought of his thick fingers anyplace on my body, his short-sleeved dress shirts with the sweaty armpits stains that never seemed to come completely out, the idea of spending one day of life forever with him made me angry. Though I loved him in God's way, I wanted to stomp a mud hole in him. I would say none of it to Leslie. I didn't even want to.

"Maybe," I say.

"I knew it," Leslie wags her finger at me. "Don't wait," she said, "don't wait."

ALL THE SAD ETC.

Christmas day 1998 and somebody decorated the lobby at Broughton Mental Hospital with a couple of wreaths smashed and bent from living at the bottom of storage boxes, a fake pine garland with ancient red bows pinned in the nettles, and a gilded candle flaking into the hard plastic holly centerpiece on the reception table.

"They went all out with the decorations, didn't they," Kim's mother, Paula, whispered. It was tacky, but an attempt at least. It had been years, over twenty, since Kim had celebrated Christmas, and though she was no longer an active Jehovah's Witness, she stayed pretty much clear of the holiday traditions. But the memory hurts, and specifics like splinters slivered their way under her skin: a tree for sure, never an expensive one, but a straggly stick fir, sad '70s elves with pinched faces and glued-on felt clothes, the year the angel-hair-fiberglass tinsel got in the laundry basket and made everyone desperate, s*cratch me please* on the lips of every family member, forever allying Christmas with inappropriate itching. But the ornaments and decorations were only part of the Christmas-merriment equation anyway. If Kim could get away with a few errant thoughts about poverty-laced Christmases, she'd be fine, more than fine. Unfortunately, the gooey nostalgia of the holiday wore her down, wiggled its way into the cracks of her resistance. Not since she was eleven years old had Kim had a tree or stocking, or glowing plastic reindeer in the yard, but the spirit, the mood of the thing, was a killer. Muzak carols. Slick magazines with scenes of fire-roaring togetherness, dinner tables decked out and glittering like whores. Smiling multigenerational families. In recent years, Kim'd found herself wondering what it would hurt to have a wreath, a few twinkle lights, some of the glow that obviously pulled in love like a gravitational force. Why not give a few gifts? Take a few? Sign up to be a Secret Santa at work? Stop standing outside the window looking in?

The problem was Kim was post–Jehovah's Witness but post-post-Christmas and the tug of celebrating was just as strong as the yank of guilt for coveting that well-appointed pagan tree. Kim didn't pretend that Christmas meant the same to her as to a lot of other people, but it wasn't fair that her brother was in a mental hospital on the happiest day of the year. It wasn't fair that she had to be there, too. That the world doesn't owe her anything, Kim was well aware, but you still keep the hope, beyond the clear evidence of reality that some fine morning, things will level out just like the good book says and you will see the unmistakable Maker's mark of design and intention on what you normally just called suffering.

The hospital-lobby room didn't need much decoration to look grand. Paintings of what had to be benefactors, maybe doctors, surrounded by heavy upholstered furniture, castle or mafia big. All to try to fool you that you were in some other place. Only the gated booth, like a bank-teller's window in a western, suggested the room was anything but a fancy reception area at the admissions office of State U.

"Merry Christmas," the man in the booth said, grinning in greeting.

"Thank you," Kim said. Paula said nothing.

"I'm Frank. Did you have a big Christmas?"

"Big as usual," Paula said and winked at Kim at their old inside joke. No Christmas multiplied by 1000 is still zero Christmas.

"We're here to see Douglas Perkins please," Kim said.

The man reached to his computer, the monitor taking up most of the open space on the narrow desk. "Just one second," he said. "Okay, not in there, but just one minute," he smiled at the women and started to riffle through a large stack of papers held together with large black clips. *Maybe he won't be here at all. Maybe this is all a mistake,* Kim thought.

"Okay, here we go, ladies. Sorry about that. Here he is right here. Ward D. What you do is go upstairs," Frank pointed to a door Kim hadn't noticed on the side of the room. "Wait I'll just show you; it's tricky." Frank pulled out a single key on a shoestring and locked the door of the tiny office behind him. Kim and her mother followed. Outside the hospital reception area was the vision of the place Kim had expected: a courtyard area with nothing but concrete the color of dull gray, pigeon color, surrounded by white buildings that evoked less the idea of cleanliness than of denial. The man gave Paula and Kim instructions to the ward and left them at the door to the building.

"We'd have never found this place without him," Kim said, more to hear herself talk than anything, though she was sure her mother was thinking exactly the same thing.

"Okay," Paula sighed and led Kim to the elevator. Neither of them expected the gigantic service elevator, and though there was plenty of room, they stood side by side, their arms touching. In the coming days, Kim would realize that elevator was made big enough for a stretcher. It was a hospital, after all, though that idea didn't occur to her then.

The elevator trip was a short one, just to the fourth floor, but the door took its time opening. Kim stepped forward to pull the doors apart. "Give it a minute, Kim," Paula said.

Kim stood back with her mother, embarrassed at her panic. She straightened her posture, steeled her face, tried to impersonate a calm she didn't feel. The hospital was the family joke. *Keep that up and they'll take you to Broughton. Keep thinking like that, they've got room at Broughton.* And a few of them were unlucky and crazy enough for the prophecy to come true. Calvin who remembered everything he was ever told: dates, names, the number of times you said a certain word in a conversation. Dead now, or he'd still be there. Arthur who wrote Bible verses in spray paint on his tiny trailer. The same Arthur who would come to your basement and remove the black snakes that took up residence there. Kim remembered waiting in the living room, the velvet furniture pushed against the wall, playing on the floor because her mother was afraid to let her play outside. They all waited to see Arthur through the picture window, the giant black snake coiled like a question mark from his brown hand, his face a picture of triumph.

Those men weren't Douglas, Kim thought. They had nothing to do with her brother. Paula led the way out of the elevator, and the two of them walked through double doors as directed, to a hallway swollen on one end to accommodate a Ping-Pong table, four folding chairs, and a spindly Christmas tree with a few wrapped gifts that Kim didn't need to shake to know were empty, several brown and white stuffed bears, the biggest one in a Santa's hat. At the other end of the hall, a large white woman sat behind a high desk like at a motel. "I'm going to ask for him," Paula said. Kim waited in front of the tree and raised her head to the high windows that let in nothing of the outside but light. Without her permission, she started to cry.

"Don't let him see you," her mother hissed. "Stop or go outside."

Kim was annoyed and wanted to lash out at her mother, but she was right. *This is not about you. This was treatment. Medicine. This is not about you.* Kim couldn't deny this situation was far better than Douglas' room in the abandoned family home, the walls polka-dotted with holes he'd smashed into the drywall, sad dirty words penciled and crayoned in all the negative spaces, the stench of piss slapping you to attention, sheets and a thin blanket stiff with it on the floor. Kim had cleaned the room wearing a mask and gloves, working in clothes she would have no choice but to throw away. She bought him space heaters he sold or threw away. Kim had wanted to ask him what he did with them but feared what he might say. Once, he'd told her about the voices that spoke to him. Voices that never encouraged or said something positive: *you look good in that turtleneck, learn a trade,* but only hissed harsh, destructive, ridiculous talk. They told Douglas he had to find a special sword. They said, *drop your pants, there's a woman.* They said nothing mattered. Douglas had told Kim he was four hundred years old. "No, you're not," she'd pleaded. "Douglas, listen to me, I remember when you were born." Douglas had patted her hand, like it hurt him that Kim couldn't understand even the simplest truth. All of that and Kim did not cry. Now at the moment of treatment, she cannot stop.

By the time Kim returns to the hallway room, Paula and Douglas have already set up the backgammon board. Besides the lady at the counter, they are the only ones in the lobby. On Christmas Day, Kim had thought they'd be bumping shoulders with dozens of family and friends, so many that they'd huddle to each other trying to hear their own private conversations. She imagined people on their way somewhere else, happy for the holiday and the weather that permitted just a thin little jacket for warmth, but still stopping for a minute.

Douglas was wearing a sweat suit like the one that the hospital had given all the patients. Kim had wanted him to look good. It was selfish, she knew that was selfish, but if he looked okay, good hair and clothes, teeth brushed, not drunk looking or unfocused from the medicine, then people wouldn't think he was so far gone.

"Hey," Kim said and Douglas raised his hand up in greeting, his movements slowed from the medicine so he looked like he was reaching for something just in front of him. But his eyes were glad, and his curly hair was spiked in different directions, uncombed but clean. Kim remembered when Douglas had tried to get his hair to hang in dreadlocks, but the texture was too fine, and short worms of it twisted off everywhere.

"What's up?" Kim hugged Douglas awkwardly from her standing position.

Douglas shrugged and turned his attention back to the backgammon board. Kim thought that she would give anything, anything at all to be out of Ward D, in the open December air. She wondered if Douglas felt the same.

"Are you doing okay?" Kim said.

"Yes," Douglas nodded.

"Okay, great," Kim said, trying to think of something to add.

"You know it's Christmas?"

Kim saw her mother glare in her direction. What did their family care about Christmas?

"Douglas, have you had lunch?" Paula said, trying to move the conversation in another direction.

Douglas nodded, "They have good food here. The best in the world."

Kim started to laugh until she recognized

Douglas wasn't making a joke. Under the billows of the sweat pants, she saw he'd gained weight. In the less than a month he'd been there, he looked to have gained twenty pounds. Kim knew it wasn't all about eating — the medicine contributed to the weight — but she couldn't get over the fact that even Douglas' body was conspiring to turn him into another person, a man Kim wasn't sure she'd recognize on the street.

"You want to play Ping-Pong?"

"Okay," Douglas said.

Kim found the paddles and a slightly dented ball under the Christmas tree. "Ready?" she said. Douglas stood on the other side of the Ping-Pong table standing dead center, limber as a rock. Kim hit the first ball over the net. The dent made the ball bounce in unexpected directions, but it didn't matter. Douglas, with slow reactions, swung his paddle long after the ball pinged onto the polished linoleum floor, one time, four times, every time. Kim will feel this moment again, she will be in line at the Empire State Building alone, in the middle of a crowd of tourists, their padded winter coats on all sides, their excited conversations peppering the air, when she will remember this very day and wail like a dog, tourists receding from her like shedding skin, like her heartache was contagious.

"You just need another ball," Paula said. "Next time we'll bring one."

Douglas sat down back in front of the backgammon board.

"We could go for a ride?" Kim said. Douglas brightened at the idea and looked up from the backgammon board.

"Don't be thoughtless," Paula said. "We can't do any such thing," she said and glared in Kim's direction.

A middle-aged white man strolled toward the Ping-Pong table but stopped in front of them. "Hello and merry Christmas," he said. He walked with purpose, no shuffling, his eyes were bright and not glassed over. He could pass.

"Yeah, it's cold," the man dug his hands into his pocket as if to prove it. "But the sun is out, that's what matters. Nice to meet you," he said and walked back to where he came from.

"Do you know him?" Kim said to Douglas. Douglas said nothing but shook his head *no*. Douglas moved the backgammon pieces as Paula kept up her cheerful chatter. Kim had dreaded witnessing Paula's breakdown, had thought it a promise. But not that day. Kim wished she'd told her mother she couldn't go or wouldn't go and had stayed in her apartment, maybe seen her boyfriend until he was summoned by his own family or even just stayed in bed with the television and a book and enjoyed the imagined Christmas of the family she created. Her imaginary Perkins family bulged out of a modest home, two boys and a girl. Their living room was full of their backpacks and coats, shoes in careless piles, magazines scattered like confetti on the carpeted floor. *Make yourself a sandwich* was scribbled on a coffee-stained edge of a note as they wait for the turkey to cook. The mayo was left out again, crumbs fallen from plates and from the mouths of people thick in conversations. But the best part of the dream: all the family rushing in different directions, "Be back for dinner," they said. And they all were.

The middle-aged man returned to their group with a decorated paper plate in his hand. "Here you are," he said, handing Kim the card. The man had glued a remnant from a store-bought card to a cheap, fluted paper plate and stapled a glittered silver snowflake to the other side. A mother of a small child would accept this card with an exaggerated face of delight.

"Thank you," Kim said, avoiding the man's eyes. He waited just out of arm's reach but did not leave. "I really like it," she said. "Thank you." Kim felt a hesitation in the man that felt like disappointment surrounded him. "Did you make this?" she said.

"I like you," the man said, though his face looked like he'd just heard bad news.

"Thanks."

"Okay," the man nodded.

"Okay," Kim said. She thought he would walk back to his room the way he had before, but instead he kneeled just in front of the little Christmas tree and arranged the stuffed bears from smallest to largest, sat each one of them up and alert, stood back to survey his work, and finally fluffed the bears' cheap fur like they were pillows. Kim thought that she had never seen anything so ridiculous and so funny and for a second she struggled to keep the giggle building in her belly quiet. Kim glanced at her mother who watched the man just as intently and flashed a quick conspiratorial grin in her daughter's direction. But only for a second. The sharp vision of Douglas' face screwed into concentration on one then the other bouncing Ping-Pong ball, his arm swinging at what he must have believed was lighting speed, his face a mask of indecipherable, heavily medicated emotion. How hilarious that would be to somebody who didn't give a damn about him. How those young or lucky or both would watch and laugh and laugh, wipe away delirious tears from their innocent faces.

The man slapped his hands together, finished, and chose the largest bear with the sewed-on Santa hat, picked him up gently like you might a child, held his stubby fingerless hand, and without a glance or comment in Kim's direction went back down the hall.

Paula checked, just to be sure they would not be permitted to go for a drive. Douglas will be leaving the hospital in two weeks, with medicine, with plans for counseling and would come out the other end, right as rain. That's what Kim told him and she had no choice but to believe it. 'Tis the season. Didn't the songs say that everything could spin into place, home was just over the river, a shining star, just look up and witness for yourself the unlikely settling into the obvious. Why not the life-changing event? Why not the miraculous materializing like magic, like an answered prayer before your very eyes?

"Well, baby, we should probably get going," Paula said, packing the backgammon board and pieces. "We've got a haul back home from here."

"Okay," Douglas said and stood up to leave. "Bye," he said.

"Wait," Kim said, not sure what to else to do. Everything was moving too fast. "Are you leaving?"

Douglas looked at Kim and shrugged his shoulders.

The gesture was so right it made Kim laugh loud, her echoing gasps taking up all the space in the room.

"Stop it," Paula said to Kim, her hands balled into fists, "just stop."

WELCOME TO THE CITY OF DREAMS

In the morning early my mother had reached her hand to mine across the vinyl of the car seat. I'd pretended I didn't see. I didn't want her to know I was interested. Mama could always sell her enthusiasm with a gesture or touch. I didn't want to be that easy.

"Tash, in the city you can be anything you want," Mama said.

I didn't know it, but I believed that Mama did. We could be anything.

Mama slowed the red Nova at the sign: Forest Acres: Raleigh, North Carolina. As we drove in, I saw what looked like hundreds, but turned out to be dozens of apartments, single story, painted gray and white on razed clay. This is the way city people lived. Sophisticated people. Not dirtroaders like us, not spread out in hick, nothing towns, but all together and connected, sharing walls in identical houses. My mother guided the car to our spot in front of unit 116.

"Get your brother," she whispered and opened the car's tank-sized door. She gathered a garbage bag full of necessities. Gary had slept most of the three-hour trip. Suited me. I liked him best asleep, even when he was a baby; I'd watch him or suck on his downy ear. In many years from that day, Gary will be asleep in the back of my Honda, his cheek pressed against the circular door handle. He'd wake up to a bright open field in Allegheny County, decorated by my friends with balloons and grocery-store bouquets.

"You're getting married," he'd say, like that was the first he'd heard of it.

Mama fumbled with the key and the overstuffed bag. Instead of rushing in the door, she turned to us and smiled. *It's okay,* her grin said, *we've arrived.*

When I remember her walking those few steps from the car, starting her new life with us, I imagine her different, a generation removed, a fifties housewife with an elegant bun, the hem of her sheath dress hovering just around the knee. But the mind plays tricks. Mama was a seventies woman, fresh-faced and young with hip-huggers and a daisy print polyester shirt, green eye shadow to her brows.

Gary and I entered the apartment behind Mama like moon walkers, our steps big and deliberate. We had never moved anywhere before and had never seen the nakedness of empty rooms. "Don't worry, we'll get stuff," Mama tossed off like the insulation of things was something she'd never considered important.

"Stay here," she said and went back out to the car for the rest of what we'd salvaged from home this morning. We'd packed all we could get into trash bags. Only the necessities, panties, shirts, nightgowns, we stuffed as Mama conducted and raced around the house trying to remember what we had to have. "Faster," she'd said again and again, making us panic and scared to get it wrong and have to start again. But this was no drill. Mama had been secretive for days at least, stretching the already long cord of the wall phone down the hall from the kitchen and into the bathroom. Through the crack between the cord and the door-jamb I could see her sitting on the toilet, waving her free hand, her words eaten up by the water she ran in the sink. When she came out, she wanted to talk, I knew it, but she wouldn't. Gary and I would be dragging into school, our homeroom teachers looking grim — *if I have to be on time, you do, too,* on their pale faces — but she didn't explain.

"This will be yours and Gary's room. It's the biggest one," Mama whispered to me. I was supposed to be impressed. I'd always wanted my own room. My best friend back home had one, but she was an only child. Things were different for them. Sharing this biggest room in the apartment was my mother's olive branch to me, the only gift she had to offer.

My mother walked to the end of the hall, running her fingers behind her. Her hand was shaking, her white-frosted nails tapping, betraying what I didn't see in her face. "What a nice color this taupe," she said. "We'll need to get some taupe drapes to match, don't you think?"

I didn't know where my mother got the word *taupe,* but I hated it. I wanted to tell her that she was lying, that she never said *taupe* before. I wanted to scream it at her to stop the singing in her voice. I had to put my finger to my own lips, squeeze my eyes shut tight to keep from screaming, *tan, tan, tan.*

The tour done, we didn't know what else to do. The events of the day had made us tentative and strange together. Anything

140

could happen. We hung close to Mama. Kept her in our sights.

Mama found our heavy yellow phone and plugged it up in her bedroom. Gary and I sat around it like adoring magi. The phone made us all more civilized, though it did look lonely on the floor by itself, Daddy's childish lettering *Alexander* in the circle on the rotary dial. Our phone number for years *758–9349* underneath. Mama tried it, put the receiver to her ear. "Nothing yet," she chirped, a little calmer now it seemed that she'd found something to do.

"Mama, can we get two phones? Another one, I mean?" I hadn't meant to sound like such a child or to get caught up in my mother's excitement, but I'd inadvertently done both.

"Two phones?" my mother laughed, a magician on the precipice of an even greater trick. "Tomorrow," she whispered, "we'll be ready to talk to the world." That's how she made the most mundane things seem like a wonder.

That first night we didn't have a television or radio in the apartment, so Mama and I read to each other. Mama loved self-help magazines, anything to make us thriftier, more beautiful, our lives as neat and manageable as the white models on the pages.

"Make a mask from honey and oatmeal that will get rid of those bumps," Mama said, pointing to the headline and the peach-faced model on the page. I felt the outbreaks of tiny whiteheads on my forehead and chin. I feared their spread more than anything.

"Give me one," Mama said, letting the slick magazine fall in a heap over her crossed legs.

"A little table salt will get out red-wine stains," I mumbled, still worrying about my face, wondering if the bumps were that visible. Mama's said that pimples don't show so much on brown-skinned people. "What if you had pink skin?" she'd said. "You'd be a mess."

"Enunciate, Tasha, what does your magazine say about wine?"

I read slowly and precisely. I wanted Mama to know I was mocking her a little. *"Pour a little table salt on a red-wine spill for easy cleanup.* Okay? Satisfied?"

I'd never seen any wine in our house. We didn't have wine glasses that I knew of. Sometimes when my mother and father had their friends around or Daddy'd play cards, I'd watch my mother take measured sips of beer from wide-mouth green bottles. She'd hold the bottle like a princess, not like the

142

other wives who gulped like men, their throats bobbing and eager. Mama never finished the whole beer. Small as the bottle was, she'd make sure to leave a ring of fluid at the bottom, politely leaving some behind, proving if only to herself, *I've got plenty.* Mama had her rules.

Daddy had rules, too. He wouldn't allow the wet bottoms of the beer to touch his kitchen table he'd salvaged from Plant 3. He said that the tabletop alone would cost hundreds of dollars if somebody hadn't forced the edge into the saw blade, killed the rhythm of the wood.

"You never drunk any wine. What do you care?" I said with more venom than I actually felt.

"Well, who knows what I'll do now," my mother said, picking up her magazine again. She didn't seem irritated with me like she could sometimes. She was being sweet today, but her sweetness scared me. I wanted her to treat me like a child and a nobody, and then I'd know what to do.

Mama motioned for me to help her with Gary, lead his sloppy body to the pile of blankets in our room. He whimpered a little, questioning if the full-throat cry was worth it, then he decided against it and went back to sleep.

"Want to sleep in the living room?" Mama said.

I nodded, not trusting my voice to hold steady.

"Beds will be the first thing we'll get, Tash," Mama said, shrugging her shoulders in what looked like embarrassment. That was the worst. I didn't want to see her anything but sure.

Mama and I sat on the floor, our backs against the wall. We read our magazines a couple of times, until Mama decided we should sleep. The solitude of the room, new plastic blinds, the walls, and the tan carpet, all of it fit for a county hospital, with so little personality in so much light. Through the windows, the street lamps shone, and I felt exposed and microscopic. I could feel God examining me to determine disease. In Millsap, our home on our dirt road, we didn't have a single street lamp. Not one. So the night never eased or seeped in but descended like a warehouse door. At home after dark, I couldn't see my own hand waving in the air over my head.

Gary's heavy, sleep-thick breathing like a baby or a fat man was audible all the way in the living room. My mother only pretended to sleep. Her taut waiting curved her back in an awkward bow. She wouldn't go unless she thought I was asleep. I knew that. After a while she stood up and shook the thin blue blanket from her legs and walked out the front door. The blue light from the lamp flooded the room. The cavalry had come, I was found. The rescuers had finally arrived at the well we'd all fallen into. I waited until I heard the click of the car handle and the secure sound of the door closing on its frame. My mother sat behind the wheel, her hands like a child at play. She rested her head on the car seat almost reclining. I'd stand at the window, see her black silhouette. As long as I could I'd make sure she wouldn't leave. Did she know how easy it would be to turn the key all the way, back the few yards from the parking space and drive away?

"I have to get a job," Mama said. She'd saved enough money from her job back home to get us the apartment, but she didn't have much extra.

"Should we be buying doughnuts and things?" I said, looking at the expensive carton of orange juice my mother brought back from the store. We never got the name brands.

"Breakfast is the most important meal of the day," Mama smiled into her cup of coffee. "We can worry about it later."

Mama had already gotten showered and dressed by the time I woke up. She was going out for a couple of hours to find a job, any job.

"You're going to like it here, Tash. A big place like this, you can have everything you ever wanted."

I thought everything sounded very good. But I was wiping my icing-coated fingers on the same shirt I had on the day before. Everything seemed far away.

"Don't open this door for nobody. And if you go outside, make sure you take this key," Mama pointed to the kitchen counter. "Or leave the door open. What have we got to steal?"

I nodded, sipped my juice. I didn't want Mama to go. I was afraid of this new place, afraid of being in all this nothing by myself.

Mama had been gone maybe an hour when Gary and I decided to go outside. I picked up the key from the counter, and we walked slowly outside into the grass, like visitors.

"Let's just walk to the end of the curve along here," I said. We walked around the block, looking for kids, though we didn't say so to each other. If there were kids around, they'd all be in school for hours still. I was already forgetting about the routine, my classroom, the cheerful bulletin boards, the small wooden desks, light-green commercial-grade carpet on the concrete floors, everything distant like it had all happened to someone else in another generation. I hadn't been to school in two days, which wasn't so ridiculous, but I hadn't talked to any of my friends. They would have to wonder why I didn't answer my phone or why I didn't call. I thought they were probably jealous. I was on an adventure. Maybe Mama knew more about how life is lived in cities than she did in the country and all she needed was a chance to get out of the life that was holding her back, making her just a pretty face in a hick town. Maybe she had plans for me, too.

No one back home would worry. In my childhood, people didn't go missing, here now and gone forever. Later when I learned more, when the world changed and women, children, even men sometimes were lost in just one day, never seen again on earth, people took notice when someone didn't show up. But nobody thought that way in 1975. Besides, Mama's best friend Trina probably knew everything, and I know she would waste no time telling. I'd heard Trina say many times that if she thought she could do better than Little George she'd be gone in a minute. She'd said she would start all over somewhere easy as pie. Like life is a series of decisions for better or worse like the game you play with children. You hold your fists in front of you, where is it, the left or right hand? Either way, win or lose, didn't matter, it was only a penny.

We'd seen just a few people getting into cars or driving along the road, but not a single child. I reached into my pocket for the key, but it was gone. At our house in Millsap, at least one window was always unlocked. Once when Mama lost her key, she boosted me into the house. I crossed Gary's dark bedroom, excited but afraid that some object would suddenly take on life or be someplace it shouldn't. I'd felt in front of me with Frankenstein arms to the back door; ready to save the waiting family.

"Okay, Gary, I need you to help me find the key."

"What key? I ain't got a key?"

"I know you don't," I said, feeling my voice thicken. "I had it, and now I can't find it. You have to help me. Let's start walking where we were, okay?"

"Just bust the window," Gary said, kicking his shoe against the curb. "I don't want to walk anymore."

On the side of the apartment, the windows were the slide kind, not the up and down we were used to, and they were high. I tried to boost Gary but he couldn't reach what we were both sure was a locked window.

"Okay then, you stay right here," I said pointing my finger at Gary. I walked around to where we'd just been. The key could be anywhere.

"What we have to do is sit out here until Mama comes," I said, feeling my mother's fake cheerfulness on my face.

"Let's just bust one," Gary whined. I wanted to agree. If Gary broke the window, it wouldn't be so bad. He would be forgiven. Why we wanted to get inside I can't imagine. The apartment creaked with emptiness. The few items looked like something forgotten or leftover. The outside should have comforted us and probably it would have if we could have recognized it. But this outside had no trees, a big menacing sky without the interruption of hills, young grass that would never take root in places. We sat in front of the door too defeated to play games.

"Who are ya'll?" said an older woman, her fuzz of white hair pulled back into a bun at the nape of her neck, her face doughy and full.

"We just moved here," I said. "We just got

149

here." I could see over the woman's shoulder, her big couch, console television and on the wall a painting of Jesus with a staff leading fluffy sheep. Clustered around Jesus were a dozen or so school pictures of homely children.

"Why are ya'll sitting out here?"

"We're locked out," Gary said. I could have smacked him right then. Everybody didn't need to know our business.

"All right then," the woman glared at us without speaking, like she would be watching our every move.

As soon as Mama came, I was so relieved I could have cried. The day could change for us. Her presence was proof. Mama wasn't smiling. Her hair had fallen around her face, and she'd taken off the jacket to her good suit.

"I can't trust you for a minute," she yelled. "You've got a whole new life and you just waste it," she said over her shoulder while she and Gary went inside. Gary closed the door behind him. I could wait. I wanted to tell Mama I'd put the key in my pocket, but it was gone. I wanted to promise something, but I couldn't imagine what. But I knew she wasn't ready to care, and right now it was best if she thought I suffered. I would stay outside until I died, until the weather or starvation killed me. She could stand some suffering, too.

The phone rang for the first time at the apartment. I just knew it was Daddy. I had expected him to come to the door any minute. I almost thought I heard his heavy step that morning. He couldn't know where we were. Could he? But I couldn't shake the idea that he would find out somehow. But it wasn't Daddy. Mama ducked her head to protect her words, a smile I didn't recognize on half of her lips.

"Who was that, Mama?" I said as my mother closed the bathroom door. She pretended she hadn't heard me and turned on the water to the sink, rummaged through her pocketbook, the click of the plastic compact falling to the floor.

"Mama," I yelled. "Who called?" I pressed my ear against the door to listen for Mama's sigh or the quick stop of her activity that meant she was angry and I'd gone too far.

"Just a friend. Don't be so nosy."

In the living room, Gary'd found a board game and had made up a version that involved throwing the game's instruction cards on the empty board.

"Get the door," Mama yelled from the bathroom. Gary jumped up to open it for a man I'd seen before, somebody from home. Our washing machine had broken down months before, and Mama had to go to the Whistle Clean Laundromat at the crossroads. Mama never did anything without the children, so we all packed in the Nova around the stinky clothes, breathing the fumes from the detergent that always managed to spill on the floorboard. I hated the Laundromat and feared my friends would see me in there putting clothes in those common washers, feeding the dimes into the machines. If anyone I knew saw me, I was going to say that our machine broke the night before. Gary didn't mind the place, but he minded little. Instead he entertained himself with the spinning clothes and long-slick tables to race his Matchbox cars. The man in our apartment had been there when we were. Not just once. A part of the mystery clicked into place.

"Gary, you and Tash say hello to my friend, Reggie," Mama said. "Say something."

"Wait one second," Reggie said and ran out to his car, a portable television under his arm.

"I bet ya'll miss this, don't you?"

"That is so nice, what do you say kids?"

"Thank you," Gary said and sat in front of the box, trying to find a channel with any reception.

"That is so nice," Mama said, smiling up at Reggie.

You could hardly make out anything for the snow on the screen, and the picture rolled, but Gary didn't seem to mind. I could hear the song in my mother's voice as she described the rooms to Reggie, the drapes she would buy. Reggie said little, seemingly used to my mother's plans.

"Watch television for a while. I'll be back," Mama said, and Reggie followed her out the front door.

"Where are you going?" I said to my mother, trying to fix my eyes so that Reggie was not at all in my line of sight.

"Just outside," my mother grinned.

I had known for a long time that my mother didn't love my father. I just hadn't realized until that moment that there might be consequences.

In the South, we eat liver mush. We slice

thin grainy rectangles, the thinner the better, into the laps of skillets. The meat sizzles on the grease, becomes lacy as the oil pops through. We eat crisp slices crunchy around the edges, on biscuits, with eggs. There is no liver mush in the North, not the good kind. Scrapple, liver pudding. Not the same thing. We'd come a long way from our last few meals at home. We'd had feasts with multiple courses and breads and salads and soups that my mother'd read about or looked up. Every dinner was a surprise our mother created. I breathed with great relief. Finally, the mother of my dreams. And she seemed happy, too, with her Seven-Up cake and banana-beef stew. Everything was a gift for our delight. We didn't say *delight*. But my mother seemed to wait for it, while we picked at saffron mounds and curled our forks under noncountry-fried meats. We should have given our unmitigated delight to her while she still asked for it.

The apartment smelled of the frying liver. I was tempted to fill a skillet with the meat, give each piece no room in the pan. You think you'd get more quicker that way, but it was a fiction. Each piece needed room to flip. Otherwise you'd have a scramble in the bottom of the blackened pan. It took longer this way, but it was worth it. I stood by the stove and admired that Mama took her time with each piece, standing far enough so that the pop of the hot oil couldn't reach.

"How much longer, Ma?" I asked, and Mama didn't get mad. Only our second full day in town and she'd gotten a decent job at the A&P. She was in a good mood.

"Three more minutes, maybe," she said. "Pour some juice while we're waiting. Don't spill it," she said, but there was no irritation in her voice.

"This week I'm working seven to four, but that's just for training. Next week I'll get a schedule like everyone else."

I concentrated on getting the juice in the glasses. Gary would fuss if I got more than he did.

"I could be working any time of the day," Mama continued. "I'm going to have to rely on you. Okay?"

I knew Mama wanted me to react, to say something, but I wasn't sure what.

"Who's gonna keep us then?" I asked finally.

"We'll cross that bridge when we need to," she said, putting two pieces on white bread for Gary. She cut the sandwich along the diagonal so he would have a point to hold onto. All of us got our sandwiches and sat in the living room. People I didn't recognize

155

from other apartments walked past. Car doors slammed, voices wafted from the apartments connected to ours. But we were quiet.

Rockford came on the fuzzy screen. The actor who played him had relatives in the next small town to ours. That's what they claimed anyway. Rockford had changed his name they said from Bumgarner to Garner, but he was still one of them. Garner was more Hollywood than Bumgarner any day. The episode had Meathead from *All in the Family* in it. I couldn't follow the plot very well, but I could tell by the wacky game-show music that the episode was supposed to be funny.

"I need to talk to you," Mama said.

I wanted to talk to Mama, too.

"Come here."

I sat beside her on the floor. She took my fingers, ran little circles across my knuckles and palm. I watched her face go blue then dark with the flicker from the television. Maybe if we stayed like this, what she had to say would vanish and nothing could hurt me, like I was certain she was about to do. I leaned against her bra, her sweet deodorant in my nose. I'd seen her scoop the white paste out of the cool jar and smear it under her arms, some of the cream sticking in the slight stubble of black hairs.

"You need to give Reggie a chance, okay?" Mama tightened her grip on my arm. Her head rested on mine. She paused like I was supposed to answer. Though I hadn't seen him, I knew that Reggie had stayed the night. I heard him fumbling in the hall, his deep whisper as the front lock clicked behind him.

"You'll like him."

"Why does he have to be here?" I asked into her breast. I didn't want to lose her in the moment, but I couldn't help it.

"When you get older," Mama said, measuring her words, trying to find just the right degree of motherly insistence, "you'll realize that grown people need to make decisions."

I wanted to say that I didn't like him, but I knew I couldn't. I wanted to beg her not to make me try.

"I deserve some happiness," Mama leaned up, her breath left my face. Of course I wanted my mother to be happy.

"You're just going to have to be nice to him. I don't want him to leave."

"Okay."

"Just be nice. He'll get used to you. I promise."

Rockford grinned at Meathead. The show was nearly over, and it was obvious from the music that the characters were gearing up for the last laugh when all the characters gather for the ending shot. This is how we remember them. Mama didn't get up at the commercial but returned her hot face on my head. Of course other people would love her. I had to make sure they did.

Mama woke me up to give me directions about the day. "For breakfast, listen Tash, there's doughnuts, apples, and milk. Eat the crackers, cheese, and peanut butter for lunch. I don't want this stove on. Okay?"

I stood in the entranceway to the kitchen half-listening. I walked Ma to the door, no screen, no trees, but sunlight that hit you dead in the face. Forest Acres was just off the belt line near one of the shopping centers. Poor people had nowhere to live in Raleigh anymore, and this project was the answer. At least a temporary one. A cheap fence around the complex made from untreated wood, fancy knockers to camouflage the plywood doors, stairs one summer away from rickety, and soon grass growing wild under the bottom rung of that fence. The place full. Waiting list for the apartments. Soon children will be everywhere. But we would be long gone from there before any of that happened. Right now the paint was still white, the cheap carpet in the apartments still chemical smelling and new.

"Okay, Mama," I said to her retreating figure. She left the apartment about 7:00, and I went immediately back to bed. After 11:00 I got up to Gary in the front room with a peanut-butter sandwich, a half-eaten doughnut on the carpet beside him. I joined him with my own food.

I'm not sure what time it was when we heard the key in the door, but I knew it was too early for Mama to return. Seconds later, the door swung open.

"Hey, hey, hey," Reggie said, trying to sound like Fat Albert. Gary laughed a full silly laugh like he'd just heard the funniest joke of his life. Reggie had him that easy. "Ya'll wanna help?" Reggie said, looking mostly at me. Gary walked outside with Reggie, but I waited at the door. Reggie looked young, green tank top, light blue shorts with thick white piping. He looked like a kid.

I wanted to catch my breath, to recover. In our parking space was a rusted blue truck full of junk it looked like. A short skinny woman and bald younger man were already loading things off. Reggie handed Gary a shoebox.

"You got it, man?" he asked as Gary took

the box into the apartment. The woman and the bald kid were wrestling with a mattress. They eventually let it fall over the side of the truck.

"Hey, honey," she yelled to me. "You direct us?"

"Okay." She clapped her hands together like something was decided. "This goes in your mama's room," she said, and I pointed her and the bald kid to the end of the hall. They moved lawn chairs and boxes of dishes, a beat-up brown recliner, and two garbage bags full of rags that I figured to be Reggie's clothing. They let Gary carry small things that he acted like was a big deal, like he was proud to do. He made me sick sometimes. I couldn't wait to get him alone to tell him how he was supposed to be feeling.

Reggie carried in a headboard for a single bed that looked like he'd just peeled off the cartoon stickers. It looked like his first move. If you have never seen poverty it will scare you. Junk packed because it was hard-won. Still I resented Reggie his poverty. He had nothing. At least Daddy had furniture. The table he was born on.

Reggie called the bald kid *Mr. Clean.* He was taller than Reggie but had a baby face.

Once everything was in the apartment,

the woman got herself a drink from the kitchen, plopped herself on the lounge chair with her legs spread open like a boy's.

"I'm Annie Belle, baby," she said to me. "Look here, Reggie, next time you need help don't call me." Annie Belle rubbed her hand over her face like she was pulling down a weathered brown shade. Reggie laughed at her with his mouth full of doughnut. He ate it over the open box, flakes of dried icing falling inside.

We hadn't had a chance to close the door when Mama walked in. I could tell by her expression that she wasn't sure what she was going to see. I would have been furious with the lawn chairs and unmatched dishes. We'd had nothing this morning, but at least it didn't look like we'd tried and failed so miserably. Mama peeked into the bedrooms. Our room had a single bed, but her room had a mattress on the floor.

"Oh how wonderful," she said. And I believe that she meant it. She ran to Reggie and hugged him in front of us. I tried not to show how shocked I was. Mama glanced over at me triumphantly like her prophecy of beds had come true and I was an unbeliever.

"Girl, this is a nice place, you hear me?" Annie Belle said to Ma. Annie Belle was probably only about thirty-three or four, but she seemed older, not exactly older, just road weary, like any minute her front teeth could fall out with decay, her limbs grow crooked and brittle. Mama paused for a minute. She never knew how to respond to black talk. My grandmother would smack her on the mouth if she said anything remotely Negro.

"We're lucky to be here," Mama said, looking around the boxy apartment. "There's a waiting list now." She circled her arm around Reggie's waist. And I realized then that Mama and Reggie must have made some plan together. He helped her to find this place, probably encouraged her. I couldn't see it. Reggie was skinnier than my father but no better looking. All I could see was Daddy did his Christmas shopping at the drugstore and brought home white baby dolls with ugly faces and poorly stitched clothes, Matchbox cars, not the good kind, just the ones everybody had. But we loved that junk. Christmas was about more, not value. None of us understood why Mama was so sullen when she opened her chocolate-covered cherries, the Windsong perfume and talc set with remnants of the big red sale sticker still on the box.

"Get some exercise," Mama said, gently

pushing Gary and me toward the door.

In the backyard, the clotheslines cemented into the ground looked like telephone lines stretching out the length of the complex. Our neighbor had clothes out, even her underwear, just one of the signs she was trashy, Mama said. We were bored. All this newness, and Gary and I were already out of possibilities. I wanted to make the best of it, but I just didn't feel like it. Mr. Clean came out to us, squatted in the grass, pulled two long blades to make a plait. Gary moved closer to him to see what he was doing.

"Can you make a whistle?"

"Nah," Mr. Clean said, twisting the grass into a ball.

"Yeah, me neither," Gary nodded like he'd discovered something they had in common.

"Why do they call you *Mr. Clean?*" Gary stared at Mr. Clean's head.

"My hair started coming out, and I had to get my head shaved."

I didn't want to call him Mr. Clean, it seemed mean. My mother would never use degrading nicknames, even when people asked her to.

"What's your real name?"

"Tyler. You ask a lot of question, don't you?"

Gary ducked his head, embarrassed for his interest.

"I like Mr. Clean," Gary said.

"You want to swing? I can swing you easy." Gary jumped up from the grass like he'd been chosen for a space mission.

"Yeah, man."

Mr. Clean grabbed Gary by the ankle and wrist, circled round and round with him, raising and lowering Gary's body in midair. Gary giggled, leaving trails of spit on his face. Mr. Clean finally put him on the grass.

"I'm drunk," Gary giggled, trying to get up but staggering each time to the ground.

"I can swing you, too," Mr. Clean said.

"Okay."

Mr. Clean put his calloused hands on my arm and leg. His skin was dry, his fingers and palms ashy. His grip hurt a little like an Indian burn. But for a moment or two, I was in flight, the world swinging in a blur, the warm May air in my face, making my eyes water. Mr. Clean tried to put me down gently, but I landed on my chin in a spot of red clay. It hurt but somehow was worth it. I wanted to ask Mr. Clean to take me in the air again. I wanted to feel the weight lifting off of me — his hands, my limbs as I floated, his eyes wide watching me spin. At the curb I noticed a little girl, maybe my age, maybe as old as twelve. It was hard to tell. She was tall but no breast buds or hips. I always noticed that when I saw a new kid. Did she or didn't she? The white girl tried to look like she wasn't watching; she wanted to play.

"You want to swing?" Mr. Clean said to the girl.

"Okay," she shrugged, pretending not to be especially interested.

"What's your name?" I said. I wanted her to know that I was in charge here.

"Sela McAllister."

Sela was taller and heavier than either Gary or I was, and Mr. Clean couldn't get her as high, but she still looked beautiful. Her face still and composed, her eyes closed, a stern look for a little girl.

"Tasha," Mama yelled from the doorway. "Dinner."

"We've got to go," I said to Sela. "Do you want something to eat?" I knew Mama would kill me for inviting someone, but I was hungry for child talk with a girl, any girl. I'd asked Sela before I even remembered that she would see the ugly lawn chairs inside, not even a kitchen table.

"I've got to go," she said like she could

165

hardly care at all, and I watched her run to her apartment around the circle. There have been many heartbreaks in my life, sorry men, worthless jobs, but the first one I can remember is watching Sela's pale legs fly upwards, pound one after the other on the blacktop, her dark thin hair swinging behind her. My mother calling again and again.

"Come on," Reggie said, motioning to Mama from the door, "come outside." Mama shot me a look but didn't say anything. I willed my face to look undisturbed.

Gary and I stayed up late. We both wanted to see Johnny Carson, and neither of us had ever been up past the introductory music.

"Go splash water on your face," I told Gary, but it was too late. His head was already jerking forward, losing the fight to sleep.

The adults came back into the apartment. I thought Mama was feeling sick, her face drawn like she'd been scared, but I quickly realized that she was trying not to laugh.

Mama shook Gary's arm. "Go to bed," she whispered, and Gary staggered up, a dopey look on his face. I thought if I could stay quiet, I might go unnoticed. I leaned against the itchy brown recliner willing myself still.

"Put some water on it, man," Reggie laughed though he was trying not to.

"Butter will be better," Mama giggled.

Mr. Clean looked in the refrigerator. I could have told him there was no butter. He let his finger under the running water.

"You gonna be all right," Annie Belle said toward the kitchen.

"I told you to quit playing with that lighter."

"Don't make fun of him, Reggie," Mama said. Reggie and Mama sat on the floor, Mama's head in Reggie's lap, him running his finger along the inside of her arm. "I told you to quit playing with that lighter."

"I hate a fire," Annie Belle said between squint-eyed cowboy puffs of her cigarette. They say black don't crack, but her full lips crinkled at the edges as she sucked on the cigarette. "When my sister got married, about twelve years ago, I seen her dress rise up in a flame. A whole brass candlestick, about ten or twelve of them, fall over and set Ricker's Chapel on fire."

"That didn't happen," Reggie said.

"I know it didn't. I saw a future fire."

Mama hated talk about ghosts or supernatural things and ignored people who did, called them small-minded. One time a neighbor told her to put red pepper in her shoes for a safe trip. Mama could barely look the woman in the face without rolling her eyes.

"I know Pam and James had a nice wedding. Her dress didn't catch fire, like I seen, but it wasn't two, maybe three months later that the kitchen of Pam's new trailer caught fire and melted everything in it as black as tar. Everybody says they only make them trailers for looks. If a big man jumps too hard that thing will shake like an earthquake. But you still don't expect your kitchen to curl up and die like that."

Reggie put his forehead on the carpet and moaned, "Annie Belle's got powers. You got a crystal ball over there?" Reggie giggled at his joke.

"I know one damn thing, you ain't shit, ain't gonna be shit, and never was shit," Annie Belle tried not to laugh when she said it.

I stored that expression for future use. Reggie laughed, but I could see from my mother's face she wasn't sure. Reggie pressed his lips on my mother's fleshy upper arm near her underarm. I thought how I'd hate that, a man's lips in my private space, in a crook of myself like he had a right. Reggie stood up and pulled Mama into his body. She giggled and didn't look back but went outside. I would scream if I could think of any reason. But there was no mouse or spider or strange man's face at the window, nothing that I could name. "Mama," I yelled to her. "Where are you going?"

My mother slung her head back, fixed her eyes on me like she was seeing me for the first time. She turned and said nothing to me.

"How did the fire start?" Mr. Clean asked.

Annie Belle stalled a second, not sure if Mr. Clean was making fun of her. "See Pam's boyfriend, not Carlo the original one, but Derrick, left some Jiffy Pop on the stove to go out to talk to some of them shabby friends he had. I told her she ought to grab her some grass seed and some rakes and put all their rusty asses to work."

"Right, right," Mr. Clean said.

I heard Mama's trilling giggle from outside. I hadn't heard that sound in a long time, maybe never. But now that I think more about it, I couldn't remember hearing that sound before. She did seem happy. I should have been glad for her, but the cruel, little person, bitter with a long memory, was growing in my stomach, thumping loud enough for me to feel it in my chest.

Mama and Reggie didn't seem to be coming back anytime soon. I'd stayed awake but ended up missing Johnny Carson anyway. Mr. Clean wanted to watch some old black-and-white movie. He canted forward in the lawn chair, the start of stretch marks showing in the space between his shirt and shorts.

Annie Belle rested on her back, looking at the new round ceiling fixture. "Look how clean that light is," she said, pointing out the fixture to me. I looked to the ceiling.

"This place is new," I said, trying to keep the sarcasm out of my voice.

"That's what I'm saying, girl," she said. "Everything is new, the carpet, the lights, everything. Ya'll are some lucky asses."

I was exhilarated when adults talked to me like I was grown. Maybe we were lucky asses. I wanted Annie Belle to know I understood.

"Yeah, I've been lucky a few times," Annie Belle said.

"Who is that on the screen, Clean? Peter Rabbit?"

"Where you see Peter Rabbit? This ain't no cartoon."

"Clean, you know any black man named Peter?"

"Yeah."

"No, you don't," Annie Belle stretched big, her shirt lifting over her pouting stomach. "You should go on to bed," she said to me. "Your mama's fine."

I wouldn't look at Annie Belle. I wasn't worried about Mama. I was afraid of the life we were building, an unhappy, unknowable one, at least for me.

"Well, if you're not going to bed, go in the kitchen and hand me that bag of potato chips." Annie Belle arranged a blanket on the floor. I handed her the bag that was mostly just crumbs. She shook it. "This is almost too much trouble to eat," she said, picking greasy crumbs from the pads of her fingers until the bag was empty. Annie Belle then stretched out on the blanket she brought, turned her back to me. "Clean, turn that mess down," she said, "and the light. Somebody turn off that light."

It was late. Later than I could ever remember being awake. Still, Mama was not back in her bed. I grabbed a plastic tumbler and took it to the bathroom. The water gurgled over the top of the large tumbler like a fountain, but I let it run, the way I never would at home with Daddy hovering, waiting to cry out some complaint I'd feel wave first in my knees and then just behind my eyes. Daddy was not here. I could do what I wanted. I waited at the sink, listening for some evidence that Annie Belle or Mr. Clean was awake. Annie Belle had looped her body around a blanket, and Mr. Clean's thick neck was resting on his shoulder, the black-and-white figures on the television playing on his face.

"Hello," I whispered. "Hello," I said a little louder. If someone woke and saw me, they could stop me. A single stream of water leaked along my forearm into the sleeve of my shirt as I carried the tumbler from the bathroom to Mama's. I thought about taking the water with me to bed. I could use it in case of thirst, in case I woke with a cough, but I knew I wouldn't. The sheets on Mama's bed were twisted into a ball. I hated to see it. When this time comes to me in my future, I will not see the two flat sheets on the floor in a roll, the lumpy stained mattress lonesome in a boxy room. I will not see my mother's clothing or the torn condom wrapper on the side. I poured the water onto the mattress. I couldn't see it, the water soaked all the way through. I filled the tumbler again and two more times until the top of the bed was slick with it, my retreating hand left a puddle. My mother would think of me when she came to bed. That was enough for now. Gary was already asleep. I thought that I might have trouble, but I don't even remember taking off my shoes, just finding an empty space.

My mother jerked me awake, her hands on my wrists. Come here, she said pulling me into the hall.

It was still night, though barely so, and I heard few sounds, a distant car or two, but no voices. My mother held my wrists in front of her, her face twisted and tight, breathing into my face.

I can see the words on her mind, words that she can't decide whether to say.

I want her to tell me what she will not suffer. I want her to rant at me, spit flying from her lips as she explains what is what. Mama flings my wrists back to me, folds her arms over her chest. "Where do you think you're going to go?" she said and walked back into the apartment. I would have cried if I'd thought of it, but I hurried behind her, afraid she would lock the door.

"What the hell's wrong with her?" Reggie said as Mama returned to the bedroom. I didn't go back to my bed. I couldn't be sure that Reggie hadn't flooded my side. I didn't want to find out by feeling the clammy sheet on my back. The certain knowledge that my mother had chosen him.

■ ■ ■ ■

Two days later was a quiet one. Reggie left early with Annie Belle and Mr. Clean. I heard their commotion in the hall, Mama's thanks over and over.

"Tasha," Mama called.

"In a minute," I whined.

"Your daddy's coming."

I felt guilty. I was guilty. Like the time I hovered over a rusty bucket in my grandfather's basement afraid to go to the only bathroom in the darkest part of the house. I fumbled with the buttons on my pants, my hands damp from the trickle of piss I couldn't control.

Daddy must have heard about Reggie, about everything. I glanced at Mama as she washed the few tumblers and dishes, trying to see if she was nervous, too.

"Is Daddy going to be mad at us?" Gary said. The very thing I wanted to say.

"I don't know," Mama said, and she sounded like she really didn't. I could hardly stand it. Couldn't she do us the service of pretending everything was going to be fine?

Gary watched from the window.

"Get away from there. He's coming soon

enough," Mama said. But every few minutes Gary would sneak back to the window.

"Daddy," Gary yelled and ran outside. Daddy parked beside Mama's car, but before he could even get his door open, Gary was standing beside it. "Hey, baby," he said, opening the car door. "How you doing?" Daddy kissed Gary quickly on the lips.

I stood in the doorway not sure what to do.

Daddy carried Gary on his chest to the door. "You gonna say something to your daddy?" Daddy put Gary down and stretched his arm out to me. I didn't think of him as a real human being, never had, but in his arms I felt the tremble of his fingers as he gripped my shoulders.

Daddy smelled good. He was dressed in the plaid shirt I'd seen a million times. His suit pants and Sunday shoes. Even I could see he tried.

"Nora, you all right?" Daddy said, looking around the living room.

"I'm fine, Calvin," Mama said.

"Good," Daddy said.

"Ya'll okay. What have you been doing?" Daddy directed the question to Gary but watched my mother lean into the wall.

"Nothing," Gary said, rolling his eyes,

eager to confess everything.

"Good. Good."

"If you want to take the kids to eat there are plenty of places down Six Forks. The road you came in on. The kids are ready."

"I'm ready, Daddy," Gary said.

"Okay," Daddy fingered the keys and change in his pocket. "Nora, I want to talk. Can we talk a few minutes, would you do that?"

Mama pried herself from the wall, fastened her lips together. "Ya'll stay in here," she said.

"Where are they going?" Gary whispered, but I wouldn't look at him. I couldn't answer anyway. We sat on the floor and waited, neither of us comfortable to sit on Reggie's furniture. We pretended to watch television, but I turned the sound almost off, my parents conversation like the murmuring of water.

"Okay," Daddy said after a few minutes. "Come on, let's eat."

Gary and I stood up, not sure if we should stay or go.

"Go with your daddy," Mama said as she walked to her bedroom, slammed the door, even the hollow door making us all jump.

I went to sit up front in the Gran Torino, a treat I seldom experienced. I loved the black interior, clean but dingy from the red dust on our dirt road. Even the mysterious dashboard panels wearing thick plastic hoods, looking like eyelids. "Daddy, did you see my room?" Gary said.

"Yeah, I saw it," Daddy said, looking ahead.

I opened the dashboard as Gary chattered. He was a good boy. I would not always appreciate that. I riffled through the papers the way I never would have before, Daddy's obvious grief making me bold. An owner's manual, bills yellowed and crinkled like they'd once been wet, a necklace I didn't recognize broken at the latch. I couldn't remember ever looking in the dashboard before. Any other time, I was sure Daddy would have noticed and yelled, slammed the plastic door shut without warning.

Daddy stopped at Pizza King, a restaurant I didn't remember, although we were five minutes from the apartment. We took a booth near the exit sign, in what I was sure was the coziest place there. Daddy ordered us sodas and pizza, and the three of us sat, not sure what to do.

"When did Reggie come?" Daddy said, trying to make his voice sound light and unconcerned.

Gary looked at me to answer.

"I don't know," I said, but the lie fooled no one.

"That's your mama's business, right?" Daddy stirred the ice in his tea. I couldn't tell if he was being sarcastic or if I was supposed to answer.

"You like him?" Daddy said, looking out the gingham-curtained window.

"He's okay," Gary said.

"I hate him," I said, but I hadn't realized I did until I said it out loud.

"It's wrong to hate," Daddy said but seemed pleased.

"I don't really like him either," Gary said.

A white family entered the restaurant, young parents, with four little children. I wondered what we looked like to them: two kids without a mother, a divorced father? A widower? Was there anything about us that said rich, happy days?

"This don't feel right, does it?" Daddy covered the top of his head with his hands like he was being arrested. "Why did she come all the way down here?"

Gary and I stared at our pizza and picked off the pepperoni and stacked them into piles.

"Is your mama happy now? That's all I need to know." His neediness had a smell that almost gagged me.

"She might be, Daddy," though I didn't know exactly what he meant. I thought happiness was living day to day without too much trouble, I didn't know of other distinctions. Daddy leaned back in the booth.

"Ya'll are all I got," he said. "I'll come for you anywhere. You hear me?"

The woods on either side of the road were being cleared of all the top-heavy pines to make way for strip malls and restaurants, a car wash sometime soon the sign said, a future bank. All this progress happening every day, making the remaining woods look out of place, a reminder of something that just didn't exist any more. Forest Acres was quiet when we returned. Though it wasn't late, I can't remember a single person sitting on a stoop, watching a child or out for a minute of air before bed.

"Are you staying, Daddy?" Gary said.

"I'll stay a little while," Daddy hesitated a moment before opening the door to the house. Mama was on one of the folding chairs. She jumped when the door opened.

"I didn't mean to scare you, Nora," Daddy said. "I knocked."

Reggie was sitting in the brown recliner. He stood when Daddy entered. He looked nervous, his one leg scratching the other

179

heel making him look unsteady on his feet.

"Reggie," Daddy said and held out his hand to shake.

"How you doing, Calvin?"

"I'm all right, man."

Reggie didn't seem to know what to do with his hands.

"It's late. Go on to bed," Mama said to Gary and me.

"Ya'll go ahead," Daddy said putting the period on Mama's sentence like we were back home. Neither Gary or I moved.

Here is where some of the elements of the moment are vaporized and only here a few images flash into my head crystallized and complete. I know Daddy pulled a package of Camels from his shirt pocket, dangled a cigarette from his lips. I know the refrigerator motor started, a waste for just the six-pack of cheap beer, the single slices of bologna and cheese. My mother was a skinny girl in a T-shirt, her hair pulled tightly in a bun.

"You want a beer," Reggie said.

Daddy studied his nicotine-stained fingers, "Naw," he laughed. "I don't want a beer."

"You should go on, Calvin," Mama said.

"I don't have anywhere to go," Daddy laughed and flicked the ashes from his cigarette to the floor.

Mama didn't say a word but watched the ashes fall to the new carpet. More than anything that had happened yet, her silence just then told me our lives were suddenly operating by different, more complicated rules.

"Go to bed," Daddy yelled, embarrassed that he raised his voice but too tired to take it back. We did move this time, but to the other side of the room.

"Come on outside, Reggie," Daddy motioned like he was coaxing a puppy. "Come on."

Reggie looked at my mother. He didn't love her. Never had and now he never would. But that was part of what she liked. I have to give Reggie his due, he would play this thing out.

"You don't have to go, Reggie," my mother said.

"We can handle this, Nora," Daddy said gently.

"Calvin, just leave."

"I want to talk to the man. He's the kind of man I'd like to have a beer with. Ain't that right, Reggie?"

"Right, Calvin," Reggie smiled to reassure himself.

It was five days since we left home. Still

the middle of May, but every hour of it had crept around the clock. In this slow-motion life anything at all could happen. Our job it turns out was to wait for it, lean into it, hope to get a glimpse of the other side.

"Can I go with you, Daddy?" I said.

Daddy looked at me and Gary. I like to think that he hesitated, wanting better for us than what he'd planned.

"Get your stuff," he said.

"Can I go too, Daddy?" Gary said.

"Go on get your stuff."

"What are you doing?" Mama screamed. "Don't you do that, Calvin."

"This is what's happening, Nora," Daddy laughed, but there was no joy in it.

Gary and I packed as quickly as we could, the best things we could find we stuffed into pillowcases.

"Calvin," Mama grabbed Daddy's arm, "let's talk. Let's just talk. Reggie go on, now."

"Don't let me see you again," Daddy said to Reggie. "I mean it. I'll kill you," Daddy said, but his declaration sounded like a question.

"Gary, Tasha, put all that back in there," Mama yelled.

But nothing could stop us now.

"Tasha, if you leave now, don't come back,

182

you hear me?" Gary started to cry, so I couldn't. Besides, coming back to that place was the furthest thing from my mind. I wouldn't turn around. There is no way I could stand to see my mother's body rushing backward, receding from me until she vanished from my sight. I wouldn't witness that with my own eyes.

When we were in the car pulled out of the parking space, Daddy stopped. Gary and I had set our attention to the road ahead, the next day, the moment to come, but before we knew it, Daddy had jumped out of the car to his truck, a board thick as his arm in his hand pounded on the door. When Reggie opened the door, Daddy swung the board into his chest, taking Reggie's breath, standing over him like a gladiator.

We heard it was no time before Mama got rid of Reggie. We all predicted that. For a couple of years, Mama stayed in Harmony, a close-by town smaller even than our town. We saw her a few times when she'd meet Daddy in the parking lot of a Williams grocery store and we'd get into her Nova and ride, always going somewhere, spending the day like tourists.

We lost track of her after that. A cousin said she went to California with a friend.

Somebody told us she was right under our noses in Lumberton. I don't know for sure. I do know that she thinks of us. Though I doubt she could afford to spend every single day doing it. No matter what, you have to figure out how to live in the day you have, not the ones you can't get back. Soon, I may look her up, just to let her know things turned out. That she doesn't have to feel bad about anything. That life runs in different speeds depending on the situation and some times and days and moments get away from you before you really know what's what. I'd tell her that I wouldn't mind being her friend. Family ought to be able to be friends, I'd say, hoping I sounded wise and centered, like a woman with her head on straight. I wouldn't talk about missing her or sad old times, or the hours we spent explaining her to ourselves and especially not the quiet nights in the dark trying the best we knew how to remember anything she ever did or said that made us laugh.

Do You Remember the Summer of Love?

The new Best Western in Birmingham, Alabama, serves complimentary drinks until the bar closes at seven o'clock. Complimentary. That means free, without cost. Except nothing's free. To get the drinks you have to spend time in the dark, already dingy little bar at one of the four small tables littered with plastic, half-empty bowls of red-skin peanuts and pretzels (the remnants of the worst cocktail party); and behind the counter: a grisly black bartender, erupting from the brick-like linoleum like a chocolate Venus on the half shell. Nothing's free. But turns out there's plenty cheap.

Jerri tried not to think about the bar or what was turning out to be a most inauspicious beginning to her cross-country road trip and concentrated instead on the steady progress of the too-full drink to her waiting hand.

"Thank you," Jerri said and fished the

shriveled lime wedge with the stirring straw. "It's been a long day. This is just what I was needing."

The bartender nodded like he'd heard the line a hundred times. "You on vacation?"

"Black people come to Alabama for vacation?" Jerri said. The bartender looked up from his own drink, an inscrutable expression on his face. Jerri couldn't decide if he was annoyed or interested. "No offense," she said.

"I don't own Birmingham. If I did, I'd sell it."

Jerri managed a tiny hiccup chuckle to let him know she'd meant no harm. "I'm from North Carolina, like that's much better." Though she knew it was. No place in North Carolina got nicknamed *Bombingham*. "It's nice here."

Jerri had no idea if Birmingham was a nice place or not. All she'd really seen was the interstate. Even this new hotel was in a could-be-anywhere franchise ghetto on a short street full of chain restaurants, copy places, and hotels. Clean, new, but every one of them as nondescript as a roll of toilet paper and nearly as interesting. Jerri sopped up the spilled gin and tonic with a paper napkin. There had been days she'd have asked for a new drink and insisted that she'd been cheated out of half of what she'd paid for. Ah, the luxury of *free.*

"What's your name?"

The man pointed wearily to his name tag, like he was sure that Jerri had already seen it. "Boles."

"Hmm, I've never heard that before." Jerri thought the name had the pretentious, canine sound of an English butler.

"Had it all my life," Boles said, though his tone wasn't scolding. "Boles was my mama's name. So I got it."

"Boles what? What's your last name?"

"Boles."

"Boles Boles?" Jerri almost laughed but something on Boles' face stopped her. "Now you're shitting me."

"I shit you not."

Jerri nodded into her drink, turned the plastic tumbler up to get the last drops, the crackling sound of the thin plastic tumbler limber in her hand. She considered asking Boles his middle name (it couldn't be Boles, could it?), but thought she might sound mocking. "Can I have another one of these?"

Boles hesitated, seeming like he was about to object, but thought better of it and turned to the liquor bottles on the back wall. Jerri watched him carefully to make sure he didn't just pretend to add the gin.

"Well, I'm glad you like your name. I've never liked mine."

"What is it?"

"Jerri Hightower."

"Jerri, not Geraldine?"

"Nope. I was named for a high school friend of my daddy's. Boy or girl, I was going to be Jerri."

"That's an honor to have somebody's name. Don't you know that?"

"Jerry's not dead. He got twenty years for rape, but they say he didn't do it."

"Dead or not, it's still an honor."

"I guess," Jerri said, but she felt burdened. What was wrong with a Mirabelle, Antigone, a Zora? "Where's a good place to eat around here?"

"Depends on what you like."

"Simple, but not McDonald's simple."

"Papa's is good."

"Is it cheap?"

"Depends on how much money you got." Boles handed Jerri two drinks. "You might want some water."

Jerri ignored the water and felt chastised but ducked her head to hide it on her face. "What name would you be if you weren't Boles?"

"My name is Boles."

"I know, but if you weren't Boles."

"I'm not going to change my name."

Of course he wouldn't. People like Boles and Jerri didn't dream of such things. They took whatever was given and made do. But forty years ago during the summer of love, white people did it every day. You wouldn't find a Boles hanging around when Peace, Sunshine, or River slid off the lips just as easy. Not that Jerri knew about any of that first-hand. She hadn't been born until October of 1967, too late for the legendary partying, too late to get a name she didn't have to associate with hard prison time.

Jerri finished the second drink in two large gulps, the ice cubes clunking uncomfortably on her front teeth. She never drank that fast. Hardly ever. But she had been stupid for a long time. Too long, she thought, but to save her life, she couldn't figure out how to stop it. If she wasn't saying, "I can't remember," she was declaring, sloppy shouldered with a sad-lipped mouth, "I just don't know."

If there had been anyone around her to care, she would have cried, right there at a bar, but she was thirty-nine, forty too quickly and too soon and had outgrown easy tears. Once when her cheeks were still chubby with baby fat, not food fat, and the only gray hairs she detected were laughable little distractions not on her chin and ripe for the picking, she'd been a crier. Anything might set it off. Once she'd sat at her father's table, just a teenager with her little brother and father, her mother working second shift then, and just as they were passing around the beans or chicken or whatever it was, she'd burst into soap-opera tears. For a second her father and brother had stopped moving, even stopped chewing, and watched her solemn unhappiness. But quickly, her father had summed up the situation, pointing his thumb in Jerri's direction, "That's the corniest thing I ever saw."

"I'm traveling across the country to California," Jerri said, the fumes from the gin making her dizzy.

"You got people there?"

"No. It's not like that."

"What is it then?"

"I don't know. You ever heard of the summer of love?"

Boles shook his head slowly, turned his mouth downward like he smelled something offensive. "Don't believe so."

"Well," Jerri started, but she wasn't sure how to explain what she meant. "It's romantic."

"You got a man with you?"

"Not that kind of romantic."

"You know another kind?"

"I walked out on the man. It's just me."

Boles poured a splash of orange juice into his drink, the yellow liquid floated down into the clear like a handheld avalanche. "He'll be looking for you. You know that, don't you?"

"No, he won't."

"Yes, he will. A man won't let you run. Mark my words."

Jerri nodded into her drink, pretending to take in what Boles said, but she knew Doug wouldn't chase. She'd found text messages from Rob who was supposed to be his friend. Their friend. Their male friend. At first, she hadn't been able to make any sense of the messages, but like those mind-numbing magic pictures from the '80s, once she concentrated on a couple of words, the whole nasty picture shifted into focus. She wasn't angry now, not really, but at that moment, she'd felt the familiar mule kick she recognized instantly as betrayal. Had she known they were together all along? She couldn't be sure. In the best impersonation of calm and collected in her life, she'd put Doug's phone back where she'd found it and wrote him a rancid note in lunatic scribble, changed her mind and threw the note away and instead left him a balled-up piece of paper beside his phone. That Doug wouldn't understand the trash she'd left behind or even notice the wad didn't hit Jerri for days.

"That's a long time on the road, girl. I drove all that way and then to Carolina and back years ago. I had to then, but I wouldn't do it now. That's why they make planes," Boles said, forming his hands into the shape of a flapping bird.

"It's a dream. You have to live your dreams, don't you?" Jerri shook the ice cubes, liking the jingling noise. "Can I have another one of these?"

"That's a lot of liquor for you all at once."

"I'm old. I know when I'm going to be sick," Jerri said, her voice louder than she intended.

"Be careful is all I'm saying."

Jerri almost asked for two drinks, just to prove she could, but she wanted food later and was already over her limit. "I'm always careful. It's boring," she said and popped a couple of peanuts into her mouth.

"Nothing wrong with that, baby." Boles smiled. "There's a lot worse things in the world than being bored."

"You know what, Boles? I bet boredom has killed more people than all the wars put together."

Boles grabbed a soiled rag from under the counter, moved it in slow circles in front of her. "You are young, aren't you?"

Jerri's room was a hotel chain's idea of a spa retreat. It was expensive at a hundred twenty dollars, but she wanted to spend her first night on the road in as much style as she could. The bed was high and fluffy, with a large quilted mattress pad that made it look luxurious. Still Jerri swiped the comforter to the floor where it landed like a snow drift. No telling what invisible filth she had just avoided.

Beside the bed was a hard little brown loveseat, a shiny cherry-wood-look coffee table, and on the opposite wall a television on a swivel stand aimed directly in the center of the room. In what looked like a design afterthought, somebody'd placed a high-back chair and a desk along the wall opposite the sofa. Ah hope! Otherwise, who was writing anything other than a suicide note at the Best Western in Birmingham, Alabama?

Jerri took off her pants and eased into the covers, karate-chopped the extra pillow to make a remote cozy for her hand. If Doug were there, he would have rolled his eyes at her: "If all you wanted to do is watch TV we could have stayed home." Ass. She should have left him years ago. That she hadn't wanted to leave him at all was a fact Jerri wasn't ready to examine.

Nothing, nothing, reality, dating show, judge show, sports. Okay, news. Every day of the summer of 2007, you could count on some old remember-when footage from forty years back with seas of white kids, swaying and jerking to freaky atonal music. What was the neatest trick of time? That everybody looked young and earnest? Or was it that all of them to the last doe-face were stunningly gorgeous? It was impossible for Jerri to believe that they weren't all beautiful to each other. Jerri loved it, though her own youth had been preppy and buttoned down. All of her '80s friends had tried hard to look like New England Scotty dogs, clean, plaid, and adorable, all with the background of keyboard synthesized music/ electronic sounds that sounded like successive pulsing tones of a telephone.

Drugs and sex and parties and fool talk into the night? Yes, yes, and yes. But all that mess had been hidden and shameful, tucked away like the morning's first gin cached in the bowl of the chandelier. Those white kids wore their sin like a jeweled crown. Jerri watched the old days with the same yellow-tinged nostalgia she reserved for her own home movies. Never mind that after Jimi Hendrix there wasn't a black face for miles. Never mind that her own parents, far from being the free-spirit flower children from the television, had been busy trying to hide the fact of Jerri's existence until they could graduate and produce the fastest growing fetus the world has ever seen. Four mere months and it's an eight-pounder. Step right up.

Jerri woke to rapping on her door. Why was the room the color of oatmeal? Why were there paintings of pastel flowers everywhere? Why was she in a nursing home when for the life of her she couldn't remember falling asleep in one?

"Yeah?"

"It's Boles."

"What?" Jerri rushed into her pants and stumbled off the high bed to the door. "What do you want?" Without the bulk of the bar in front of him, Boles looked smaller and kinder in his too-large shirt.

"Hey, you all right?" Boles said and searched the hall behind him like he wasn't sure he'd found the right room.

"How did you know where I am?"

"I work here."

Jerri knew there was something wrong about Boles being at her door, but she couldn't pull the words together to object.

"You want to go to Papa's? I haven't eat either."

One of Jerri's socks was hanging off her foot, a clown's foot, and the other had disappeared into the bedclothes. Jerri knew without looking that her hair puffed in the back like someone had pushed her from behind. If she hadn't drunk so much and so fast she was sure that she wouldn't be putting on her shoes and finding her way out the door with Boles.

Papa's was at the edge of the downtown area in a squat warehouse building. There were no windows, no flowers, nothing to let the wanderer-by know that she was seeing a restaurant except for the large vertical sign: *Come to Papa's. Stay and Eat.* Papa's was not quaint. Jerri followed Boles into the cafeteria-style line where they were separated from cooks and servers by a high partition behind which a phalanx of stainless-steel bowls bubbled full of rich Southern foods. Sweet potatoes, cream corn, fried chicken, mashed potatoes, gravy — white and brown — stews, country-fried steak, pork chops, and that was all at first glance, happy as sweet little newborns behind the glass. Mama's here, Jerri thought.

"The pork chop is good and the greens. I always get the greens," Boles said. In this better light, Boles looked even older than Jerri had thought, at least sixty, older than her parents.

Jerri didn't want greens. Let Boles have them with his country 'Bama self. She picked the baked chicken, lima beans, fried okra, sweet potatoes, and buttermilk pie. Too much, but she hadn't eaten for hours. "I'm buying my own," she said.

"All right then." Boles shrugged.

The two of them sat at a booth near the drink machine. A white woman older than she wanted you to think brought them tea in glasses big as pitchers of beer. "Ya'll let me know if you need anything else," she said.

Jerri watched the retreating back of the waitress, a slim woman with impressive bubble curls bouncing on the tops of her shoulders. "You ever notice that in these places all the people cooking are black and the waitresses are white?"

"Did I notice?" Boles said. "You asking me if I noticed?"

The food was filling, too much, but they ate quickly like starved people.

"You better get on it, I'm way ahead," Boles said between bites of greens. "You don't put a plate of good food in front of me and expect it to sit around."

"Don't worry, I'm a good eater. It's my hobby."

Boles nodded sagely, like he'd known plenty of people with an eating hobby, no news to him. "Where do you want to go after this?"

"After this?" Jerri was surprised at the question. She hadn't considered spending the entire evening with Boles. "What do you usually do?"

Boles raised his eyebrows, pursed his lips, worrying the question with great seriousness. "Nothing."

Jerri sucked her lip, hoping she looked superior and worldly, but the truth was she mostly did nothing, too.

"Well, I can take you on back," Boles said.

Jerri knew the same familiar routine that went on in North Carolina went on everywhere. Ugly, tired people, haunted run-down restaurants, malls, and movies in cotton and buy-one-pair-get-one-free shoes. Nobody ever bothered to tell Jerri that most of life was spent just that way, going through the motions, doing the routine, trying to make it out alive from one minute to the next. Even if they'd told it, Jerri doubted that she would have believed it.

"How long you taking to get to California?"

"A month. I don't know. As long as it takes."

"You got money?"

"What would you say if I told you that I'm taking all the money I've got in the world for this trip? Every little dime I'm flushing right down the toilet."

"It's your dime baby; if you want to flush it, flush it." Boles's pressed his hand over hers. "That's life, ain't it? You don't see none of it back." Boles grinned with one side of his mouth like something was set into motion that only he understood. Even young in his best most vital days Boles must have seemed like an old man, with his half-closed eyes and slow ways, he must have worn a sense of the everyday tragic as real as the custard crust now stuck in the crease of his lip. "You look out for yourself. There's all kind of fool out there."

Years ago, Jerri had slept with a man she

only just met when she'd visited her cousin in Florida, the first and only time she'd done such a thing. As soon as she got back home, she warmed to Doug like she didn't know was possible, listened to him, waited to really hear him for the first time, loved him for sure. God keeps count. That stranger's flabby middle, his thick yellow-tipped fingers came back to her with a clarity she wouldn't have believed possible. So this was how the scale gets balanced. Jerri winced to hold back tears. She was still Baptist enough to believe that the payback you do for wrong, though inevitable, was still always a hellish surprise.

Jerri tried to slide her hand from underneath Boles's, but she couldn't budge it. She picked at her chicken with her free hand, red at the bone, careful not to look in Boles's eyes. She didn't want to see the crazy that might be on his face that she'd completely missed before.

"I'm here now. Whatever's gotta happen, gotta happen."

Boles grinned at her, then sighed like something had become resolved and clear to him. "You're all right," he said and gave her hand a friendly pat. "You're a good girl."

"I want to go back to the hotel," Jerri said.

Boles picked the last of the crumbs from

his pie with his moistened finger, as if he hadn't heard Jerri at all. "You got any kids?"

"Not that I know of," Jerri sighed.

"Wouldn't you know?"

"It's a joke, Boles."

"What's funny about that? Where I come from a joke is supposed to be funny."

"I just want to go back to the hotel. Okay?" Jerri hoped she sounded in more control that she felt.

"We're going." Boles said as he slid out from the booth, brushed his clothes of crumbs, let the paper napkin float off his lap and onto the floor.

The hotel was a few blocks from the restaurant, a five-minute trip in Boles's low-riding car. Jerri opened her door, eager to get back to her room.

"What are you rushing around for?" Boles said.

Jerri stood outside the closed car door not sure why she waited. It was hot, the air stiff and motionless already, a harbinger of the stifling summer heat to come, but Jerri saw stars bright as headlights even in that polluted night on franchise row. It was hard not to believe that it was one of those moments, when the main character looks heavenward and takes a deep cleansing breath, the night fulfilling some kind of promise she believed with new certainty would be kept.

"Let me come up with you?" Boles said, sounding like a young boy.

"I'll see you, Boles. Dinner was good. I appreciate it."

"Let me come up with you?" Boles rushed to her side of the car. "I'm not a bad man."

Jerri brushed past Boles, raised her hand in what was supposed to be a wave, but looked more like a halt. "I can see that," Jerri said. "I'm sorry. I don't care. I wish I did."

Inside the elevator, Jerri felt more alone than she had in years. Maybe Boles was on his way up to her room in the service elevator. Slow, old Boles waiting for her at her door or charging into her room with his narrow hunkered shoulder startling her in the night. Jerri reached for her phone, scrolled through the contact numbers. Who was going to help her in the world? Her mother had called twice, but no call from Doug since the day she'd left and even then all he'd wanted to know was what she was going to tell people. His indifference was an insult that she couldn't have expected. All these years later and Doug wasn't even her friend.

There were only four floors in the building, and Jerri's room was on the third. Jerri pressed the button for the fourth. The fourth floor looked exactly the same as the third floor with an iron hall table with a glass top and above a gilded mirror, looking like it would be at home either at Versailles or the elevator stops at the first through fourth floors at the Birmingham Best Western. The message couldn't be more obvious. But sweet Jesus, if nothing truly changed in your world, not even the scenery, then why did it matter so much?

When the elevator door opened, she waited and watched as the door closed again. She rode down, a minute, less, to the lobby, waited, watched the door open, then close and rode back up to the fourth floor, again, and then twice more. The last time the front-desk man, a young black man with a pouting stomach, was waiting when the door opened. Jerri gasped and startled both of them.

"You all right?"

Jerri shook her head, first *no,* then *yes.*

"I don't know what you mean, ma'am?"

"Yes," Jerri said and pretended to search through her purse for something she could wrap in her hand.

"Did you lose your key card?"

"I'm tired." Jerri snapped her pocketbook shut and smiled at the man.

"Can I help you? Can you tell me what you need?"

She would go to Louisiana the next day. She would get to California. The rest she'd figure out. "I'm okay."

The lines were busy at the dog registry, ringing off the hook like in those old black-and-white movies where the business mogul has ten black phones glossy as beetles lined on his desk: *Mr. Important here. Sell, sell!* Shelia wore her headset like the sixteen other phone operators, telling dog owners from all across the country how to fill out dog-registry papers or where to mail papers or how to get the papers they were promised and never received or how to change the spelling of the names they've chosen (you have no idea how many My Little Angles are barking around out there). Eight hours a day of "Yes, ma'am, sign your name where it says *new owner.* Right. And the former owner has to sign where it says *former owner,*" over and over again.

The lit-up switchboard excited the five-foot tyrant of a phone manager Angie. Shelia dreaded the sight of her twisted face over the short-walled cubicles, eager to catch any one of them with their phones switched to silent and staring off into space. Angie was not beloved. But none of the management staff were what you might call Sunday-dinner guests for the North Carolina locals. Southerners couldn't get used to the loud, unsmiling women, hair dyed improbable red power colors, their haughty nasal accents as they mocked their North Carolina employees. *Thaaank yew!* They teased, drawing out the vowels like taffy. Shelia spent too much time wishing all those New Yorkers had never moved the dog registry from Manhattan at all. Of course she wouldn't have a job, but she'd manage. People do. Though Shelia had started to wonder if she was actually managing or simply laying down decorative pavers on the path to crazy. There were only so many soul-stealing times you could listen to the moaning and ranting about dogs, of all things, before you were through — through, like past here, beyond that, and all the way to the other side. By Shelia's calculations, she was less than a week's worth of phone calls from her limit. She tried to explain to her fiancé Polo about it, but the wrongs she recreated sounded stupid even to her. *Suck it up. Man up,* she told herself every morning on the slow ride up to the second floor in the service elevator. National Kennel Club wasn't anybody's dream job.

"Yes, ma'am, I'm listening," Shelia said as she scooted as close to her neighbor's cube as she could. Diane had cut dozens of magazine pictures of Patrick Swayze and pinned them all over her padded walls. Shelia laughed at her, like everybody else, a grown woman, a woman on the downhill side of middle-aged at that, but she secretly kind of liked the collection, the exhibit-A evidence that somebody loved something — even if that something was ridiculous.

"He looks like a sheepdog terrier," the woman said. "For God's sake, how can you let people sell animals like this?"

"I understand, ma'am. In order for us to open a case we must have some information. Do you have a pen handy?"

Shelia heard the woman drop the phone, the squeak and pull of drawers opening.

"Go ahead," the woman snapped.

"We need pictures of your dog, the names and current addresses of the owner of the sire and dam, pictures of the sire and dam, everything you witnessed or learned about the conditions of the mating," Shelia paused for the woman to write the information down, though, of course, Shelia knew she wouldn't. The dog owners don't want leg-work, extra phone calls, and questions. They want action and they want it now. Phone magic, a little presto-chango over the fiber optics and their trembling, knock-kneed creature becomes a champion, the star of the dog show, worthy of their registry name: Prince Valiant Emperor Angle the Third.

"Conditions of the mating? Look, all I know is I've got a sheepdog body with a terrier face. I didn't pay $500 for that."

"I'm sorry, ma'am," Shelia began in a voice she hoped was sympathetic but sounded a little weary even to her. She couldn't imagine a situation that would fill her with less grief. "We will be happy to investigate."

"Investigate! How can you let people do this? Nigger in the woodpile is all I know. Now I have to foot the bill for a nigger in the woodpile."

Shelia never hung up on callers, no matter how obnoxious or abrasive, but let them wear themselves out, struggle so hard on the chain of the telephone line that the fight finally left them. She prided herself on how much trouble she could let dog mommies and daddies lay at her doorstep without a word, without one nasty word. She once talked to a man for twenty-seven minutes, more like listened to his rant, about why his beautiful collie from the pound couldn't be registered. A dog from the pound might be anybody, the bloodlines muddied with the genes of mutts and ordinary curs. You couldn't know that the dog in the pound today was the pureblood you lost the day before. You couldn't be sure. And blood should tell. For that caller Angie finally broke in on the line and in her New York way ended the madness. "I'm Angie the manager. Forget about Jiffy," she said. "You got it?"

Shelia had her own method for dealing with the foolish or ill-mannered. Her aunt had been part of the last class at the all-black high school in town and had taught Shelia the unofficial cheers the crowd used to yell from the sidelines. Their cheers were tough: *We're the blue imps, and we're slick and fine, if you mess with us we will blow your mind. We are the blue imps, super cool. You mess with us, you're a fool. My sign is Gemini. That's no lie. You mess with me, I'll black your eye.* But the one Shelia loved most wasn't a cheer at all, but a chant. Over and over again, *Ungawa, ungawa* (clap clap). *Black power, black power* (clap clap). But Shelia couldn't taste the full-vowelled sound of *ungawa ungawa* that day, only the acid-meanness, the rancid vinegar of hurt and hate stinging at the back of her throat.

"Why do I have to find out conditions of the mating? I'm the one suffering. Me," the caller sighed heavily into her phone. "Are you there?" she asked.

Shelia did not respond but let the caller hear her breath, let her hear the other conversations in the background. She wouldn't hang up, but she couldn't speak. What could she possibly say that the woman shouldn't have already learned?

"Hello! Hello! Are you there? Goddammit, answer me."

The woman's sheepdog was going crazy in the background. His pointy little face in motion from the heartbreak he sensed from his owner, showing more loyalty to her than she would ever have for him.

"Where are you?" the woman screamed.

Shelia let the caller yell, playing the odds that Angie wouldn't notice the long call and break in on the line or rush around the corner. Shelia imagined the story the woman would tell her husband later, a saga gripping only to her of the terrible, rude telephone clerk. "She hung up on me," the woman would insist, feeling the outrage all over again, while the husband would nod in understanding, not giving the first hot damn, interrupting, "But did you get the papers?"

"What's your name? Tell me. I'm going to have your pitiful little job. Do you hear me? Shit, shit, shit," the woman yelled, punctuating every word with her pounding fist.

And your little dog, too, Shelia thought and giggled into the phone.

"You're there!" The woman said, so angry she sounded like she might start sobbing. "I hate you," the woman screamed as loud as she could. "I hate you so much," she said, and the phone went dead.

After exactly an hour and eleven more calls, Shelia could take no more, grabbed her paperback and headed to the break room. Shelia had made a game of how long she could hold out before she took her fifteen minutes. But not in the last hour of the day. If you held out that long, you might not get your minutes at all. And don't even think about taking a break at your desk. Angie would bust you good for that. You had to take the trek, like a walk on a red carpet in hell, past the surly faces that glanced up at you as you crossed the airplane-hangar-sized room. Past the writers, called *correspondents*, who were the first response to the written complaints and set up cases against breeders and pet stores. Past the correspondents who dealt with claims of impure breeding and the two correspondents who responded to issues of divorce and custody of dogs — the love-gone-wrong cases. Past the women who typed the many letters the correspondents dictated into their recorders. Until finally, at the end of the building, you reached the blue door of the break room. Shelia never, ever started her fifteen minutes before she reached that door.

Only one other person was there, the weird young man who moved all the way from New York City to work in the company's loading dock.

"Hey," Shelia said. She would have been more enthusiastic, but she couldn't ever gauge the New Yorkers. Either they ignored you or acted with indignation or surprise to your greeting. A body gets tired of trying after a while, but cornered, a Southerner will greet.

"Yeah," the man said and turned his back to Shelia to watch the fascinating progress of his Pop-Tart in the microwave.

Shelia had no food. Never did. But she always carried a book. With a book you look busy, never had to wring your hands or thrust them hard in slim pockets, ashamed and idle. She would have loved a friend to

212

talk to, but there was only Wendy, the other black woman at the registry, only two years older than Shelia and a member of her original training class. But Wendy and Shelia had been late back to their desks too many times to risk it. The last time Angie had screamed at them, her hands hard on her skinny hips, "No more!" she'd yelled like a pouty little kid.

The man in the break room wore jeans today, but the North Carolinians lived for the days he broke out his skirts — not kilts, skirts, long A-line affairs that cut his hairy leg at the shin. A short guy like that didn't need a skirt that long, Shelia wanted to tell him and even considered gesturing with a karate chop across her knee. *Right here,* she'd mouth. But who knows what the man might make of it. He might think the gesture was a gang sign. Though the only gangs Shelia knew were the old-people walkers who circled Crabtree Mall, all elbows and determined lips, looking like bulldogs with switchblades.

Shelia sat near the window overlooking the enormous parking lot. Not since she was fifteen years old had she been without her own car. Now she got dropped off every morning, while Polo gunned the tinny engine, revved the car all the way up the hill to Cary Road. Fifteen minutes in the break room, ten minutes in the bathroom, five minutes adjusting her headphones, five minutes getting pamphlets to address to callers needing basic information, and, maybe if she was feeling bold, a second ten minutes in the bathroom. If she could manage these breaks she'd have only two hours and fifteen minutes to go.

Betsy, the trainer for all the new-hires, flounced into the break room. She always looked the same, front-button flowing dresses, whisking around her still-skinny legs. Probably the same dresses she wore to dog shows, the very ones she wore to lead her prize cocker spaniels around the rings. Betsy's office was full of pictures of her with one, then another sad-eyed, glossy dog with ribbons around their necks; they looked too demoralized to try to eat. Or maybe that's just how they looked to Shelia.

"Shelia!" Betsy exclaimed, the practiced look of delight on her face, "How are you?" Betsy stood in front of the refrigerator, waiting for applause. She probably was popular on the show circuit. An attractive woman in her midfifties, smiling like a debutante, her golden blonde hair, cropped in just-so layers, gleaming like wealth in the lights, her elastic face in another look of astonishment,

214

now happiness, now great and abiding concern.

"Okay," Shelia said and tried not to look long at Betsy but concentrate on her book.

"You won't believe the story I heard," Betsy took her carton of grapefruit juice from the fridge.

Shelia could not imagine a world in which she would care about Betsy's pity story, her attempt to bond with the help, let them know she was not one whit better, no sir, a regular Josephine, by God. What she succeeded in doing was proving she could force you to sit and listen to her talk.

"This weimaraner breeder, I've known her for years, had the most beautiful dogs with coats so silver they were blue. Gorgeous. Coats like you wouldn't believe."

Shelia was supposed to respond, express her disbelief at this idea of blue dogs, but she couldn't think of any way to care.

"This weekend, this rainy weekend, we all found out how they had those blue coats," Betsy lowered her head conspiratorially. "Dye. Blue dye. Nobody would have guessed it."

But Shelia knew Betsy guessed it. Guessed it and predicted it to anybody who would listen.

"People are nutty," Betsy chuckled, waiting for Shelia to chime in with her laugh. "Just nutty."

Shelia knew that if she gave Betsy a courtesy laugh she would never get rid of her and her whole break would be squandered listening to one after another of Betsy's stories. Don't look up. Don't look up. Courtesy dictated that Shelia look up.

"What are you reading?" Betsy asked, turning up the cardboard carton to get every drop of juice.

Shelia turned the worn paperback over in her hand and showed Betsy the fraying cover.

"A romance, huh? Now that's the way to pass the day," Betsy grinned.

Shelia couldn't think of any way to explain to Betsy how completely right and wrong she was. How could she tell Betsy that no romance could leave her as weak with longing as this book had? What would Betsy care that whatever it was that passed as magic in the lives of the people of Macondo was missing from hers? How could Shelia even put into words how predictable everything in her day had become: the Peanuts cup with the cheap Bics, the ripped chair no one had bothered to move from beside the entrance to the elevator, the smiling sultry face of Patrick Swayze staring at her as she found the chair at her cubicle.

"I'm not that far into it."

"Let me know how it is. I might try that myself," Betsy grinned. Shelia would not look at Betsy now. She would not look up at Betsy's face and scream with her expression that she knew that seconds after their conversation Betsy would not even remember talking to her.

"Well, I better get back," Betsy said, making a show of checking her watch, signaling to Shelia that surely her own break was over.

The Pop-Tart guy swished his hands together in triumphant finale and walked out. Betsy stood up and pretended to be interested in the magazines abandoned on a table next to the door. Shelia's only recourse was to stand up herself and follow Betsy to the door, her book nestled under her armpit.

"Shelia!" Angie screamed from across the office. "We've got calls lined up. To your desk. Now."

In high school, everyone would have laughed at the rebuke. How funny it was to see a peer get called out in front of everyone. How superior and sure it felt to see one of your own as stranded and mute as a wobbly-legged colt in a wide-open field. It would do no good to explain to Angie that she was only taking the break she was entitled to. At least none of the other telephone operators laughed. Shelia wouldn't have been able to stand that.

Even in school, when she was a kid and could be excused for thinking big, she'd dreamed safe: a good car, the light bill paid on time, food huddled in stacks in the fridge. It didn't matter that most of her classmates, especially the black ones, lived much the way she did. If pressed she could name all of the black girls in school on her fingers and toes. One of her classmates went briefly to Livingstone College. A few spent a semester or two at community college drawing out their high school days to their ridiculous limits, their old antics finally feeling too predictable even to them. The Lackey twins might be the only ones among them in good shape, but that was to be expected. Shelia had hated the twins, the way they stuck to each other like cockleburs, their rich crybaby faces always taking up all the special air in the room. The twins need a break, the twins are scared, the twins are sad or crying or annoyed. Again. Unfortunately for Shelia they always managed to be with her in the same homeroom classes. Shelia had not lacked for friends, white friends like Allison, an only child with a television in her daddy's van, or Donna, dark haired and beautiful, with straight teeth and wavy hair, though her beauty peaked at thirteen. Even a few years after high school Donna sent Shelia a clipping about the death of one of the boys they'd admired. But the Lackey twins had the gift of each other, a constant and beloved witness and narrator to their experiences. It hadn't occurred to Shelia at the time, but of course she was jealous. Who could stand that no matter what, the Lackey twins would always together be the queens of the colored-girl parade?

"National Kennel Club, may I help you?"

"I guess so. Hey, what's your name?"

"Shelia."

"Shelia? I'm Todd. You don't hear *Shelia* much anymore. You sound young for a name like that," Todd yawned dramatically into the phone, "Sorry, you don't care." Todd cleared his throat. "Hey, I need papers for my dog."

Shelia hadn't thought about her name being particularly old-fashioned, but she couldn't think of another woman within twenty years of her age who shared it. "You need papers? Really?" Shelia laughed.

"Yeah. I guess you probably hear that a lot. I just woke up. Is that obvious?"

"No, you're fine. I was just joking."

"You want me to call you back? I can call back."

Shelia paused not sure if the man were serious or not. "No, no, I'm sorry, just tired today. I can help you." Shelia picked up the National Kennel Club brochure about upcoming shows and events, the only thing close to a magazine the telephone operators were allowed to have at their desks. On the cover of the puppy guide was a small blonde child and her rottweiler pup; the dog looked to be covered in down, staring into the girl's round chubby face, love or need, a human emotion on his canine face. Maybe it was the fading light meant to dull any harsh lines or angles in the photo or maybe there was so much youth and innocence in the scene that the only conclusion was that both would soon and forever be past, but the photo made her stomach, no — a deeper place than that inside her — flutter with nervousness.

"Let's start at the beginning," Shelia said. "Where did you get your dog from?"

"Why are you so tired?"

Shelia occasionally got calls from lonely people with nothing else to do but talk to anybody foolish enough to listen. Only a few of those phone calls lasted long. In the middle of the second or third confession or anecdote, the callers heard their own silly selves and hurried the conversation, not willing to admit any longer how pathetic they had become. "I can't sleep. It's nothing."

"I hear you, but it's not nothing. I didn't sleep for eight years. Swear to God. I lost the best part of the '80s like that."

Shelia couldn't tell if the caller wanted sympathy or laughter.

"I survived pretty much okay," Todd laughed.

"What's your name again?"

"It's Todd. You don't believe it, but I didn't sleep more than forty-five minutes a day for eight years. I almost forgot about that. I was pretty messed up then. If I wasn't waiting for a check from one of my customers, I wouldn't be up right now. He was supposed to be getting paid today. I'd like to know how much of my life I've spent waiting on a check."

"You must work nights?"

"Yeah, mostly. I sell drugs. None of that hard shit. I won't sell anything I wouldn't use myself."

On the road leading to Shelia's Aunt Lou's, boys and young men lined the sides, five or six of them a night and waited for stopped cars they could run up to and hand through the window a packet of your usual. The whole process took a minute or less. Aunt Lou was a tall woman, big boned, wide hips and chest. Shelia hated that tough old Aunt Lou was afraid of the boys, afraid to come outside on her porch on the road where she'd lived her whole life. "Somebody's going to get killed up here, mark my words," Aunt Lou had said, and of course she was right, but it didn't take a crystal ball to see that vision. Shelia wanted to hate the dealers, but since she had known most of them when they were children together, hating them didn't come easy.

"Any money in it?"

"Drugs? No, no, not the way I do it."

"I've never met anybody who makes money. They talk about money all the time, but as far as I can tell it's talk."

"You can make some money, but you have to really hustle. The nuns called it years ago, I don't apply myself."

"It's never too late, Todd." Shelia tried to imagine what the man on the other end of the line looked like. He sounded young, but the voice could deceive. He sounded white, but her callers always thought she was white and were sometimes annoyed if they learned she wasn't. "Do you have a pit bull?"

"A pit bull? You got the wrong idea. I don't like to get shot at. Look, I didn't always sell. I've done lots of real things in my life. Last year I did some substitute teaching. Elementary."

"I thought about doing that."

"Don't do it. It's hell. Fifth grade is hell. They need to give teachers a house, a car, a train, a pond or something, if they stay for twenty years. Listen to this, the day I left I was in front of the class teaching, really into it, you know, and I put my foot on a chair and heard my pants split."

"Oh no."

"The kids are laughing. That's natural, right? They're eleven years old. But there's this one little kid, the little geek in the bunch who chimes up and says, 'Mr. Kessel that's okay, we all have bad days.' You should have heard the other kids. They unloaded everything they were giving to me all on him. So I said, 'Listen you pieces of shit, I go home and talk to my girlfriend about every one of you illiterates every day. Me and my girlfriend laugh our asses off about what little nothings you are.' You know what happened? All the little turds heard was *girlfriend.* 'Mr. Kessel, Mr. Kessel, you've got a girlfriend, tell us about your girlfriend.' "

"Oh my God, you didn't really cuss out a room full of fifth-graders?"

"That's not even the worst part. I said, 'Yeah, I've got a girlfriend,' and I reached in my pocket and opened my hand and said, 'here she is,' like I was getting ready to do a trick and puffed my cheeks up and blew her away. That's when I walked out."

"Why did you do that? The blowing part?"

"I don't know," Todd chuckled. "It was the first thing that came to me. It seemed right at the time."

"That's stupid. Why did you screw yourself up like that?"

"That's not what happened."

"Yes, it is!" Shelia insisted. "You didn't accomplish anything, and you lost your job."

"That's one way to look at it. I didn't see it like that," Todd paused, and the line was silent. Shelia considered apologizing, but she was right, she was sure of that. You shouldn't lose everything for nothing. That had to be law of nature.

"My daddy's been at the same job at a furniture factory for twenty-five years, and I don't think it would ever even enter his mind to piss everybody off."

"Why?"

"What do you mean *why*? He's got bills!" Shelia sputtered. "He's got to live."

"Hey, I admire that. Swear to God I do. But, I always come out okay. Easy come, easy go."

Shelia thought about telling Todd about her father's long shifts in air thick with dust too fine to see, but settled on you like a second skin, or the loud machines that sounded less angry than unsatisfied, covering over every other sound on the work floor. "Anyway, my dog's a hot dog. You couldn't pay me to take a pit bull. They'll turn on you."

"You mean a dachshund?"

"Yeah. She wags her tail, and the whole back half of her wags like a windshield wiper."

"Yeah," Shelia said, still annoyed at Todd's story, though she knew she had no right to care.

"I know, it's cute. That's the problem. She couldn't shit, and I had to squeeze her stomach like a tube of toothpaste to get it out. You think I'd do that for a dog that wasn't cute?"

Shelia laughed in a burst she was sure they must have heard in the next row of operators. She looked around for Angie. "You lie," she whispered.

"I'm serious. I'm the only drug dealer in the state of Illinois squeezing shit out of a weiner dog."

Shelia tried to draw on her desk blotter a man squeezing the long expanse of a dog's belly. She tried to capture the dog's relief, the man's sincere desire to help on his face, but her cartoon turned out looking sad and pornographic. "Okay, I should try to help you. Did you get any papers with her?"

"For Samuel? I thought that's what I was calling you for."

"Is Samuel your dog's name?"

"Yeah, you like it? I was saving it for my kid, but she came first. At least it's better than Bathsheba."

"Like the Bible, Bathsheba?"

"I don't know. All I know is when I got her she was Bathsheba."

"Bible names."

"What?"

"Those are Bible names," Shelia tried to remember the stories. Samuel and Bathsheba's stories seemed connected but that could be wrong. Bathsheba had something to do with sex or rape, what else? Shelia was irked that she could call no details to mind.

"You know your Bible," Todd laughed.

Shelia snorted, "Not really. Okay, tell me exactly what you got with Samuel? Any paperwork at all?"

"I got her from a friend of my brother's,"
Todd said, like that explained everything.
"She was my brother's friend, his girl-
friend."

"Why didn't your brother take the dog?"

"You don't want to know," Todd sang into
the phone. Shelia thought with a little prod-
ding she could hear the story, but she'd
heard it before, no need to worry with all
the cheap little details. "Why doesn't my
brother do a lot of things? Most of the time
me and him are working on who is going to
fuck up his life first. But anybody who
knows me will tell you, I wouldn't let a dog
starve to death."

"Maybe it's a cry for help," Shelia laughed.

"That's not funny," Todd said, but he
didn't sound offended.

"I know it's not," Shelia pinched her lips
to hold in the giggle. "You didn't know you
were going to get counseling and dog papers
on this call, did you?"

"You do sex, too?"

"Ha. Not for seven dollars an hour."

"I hear you. Would you do sex? Not now,
necessarily, but ever?"

"No. Are you crazy?" Shelia said, but she
had often thought that phone sex wasn't
that far from what she already did. The
constant stroking and consoling, sucking up

and flattery she did to keep the conversation moving.

"I used to think there were things I wouldn't do."

"There are things I won't do," Shelia said, but she wasn't sure what they were. "Did the friend give you any papers at all?"

"Did I hit a nerve?"

"No. God no. I'm perfectly fine."

"I bet you weren't expecting this conversation today. Did I surprise you? I like to surprise people."

"I sort of did it one time."

"What."

"A guy called doing a survey for Dr. Scholls, but I knew he wasn't. I could hear his television in the background," Shelia paused not sure why she was telling this secret to a stranger. "I told him I was wearing yellow pumps and lace ankle socks."

Shelia didn't see Wendy come up behind her and jumped when she left a note on her blotter, *pee thirty.* Shelia nodded okay and Wendy gave Shelia a thumbs up, no evidence on her face that she had heard what Shelia just said.

"I bet he shit a brick."

"What?"

"When you said that to that guy, I said I bet he shit a brick."

"It was stupid, wasting time on that guy."

"You did a public service."

"No I didn't," but Todd's assessment made Shelia feel better. "You're just saying that."

"I know what I'm talking about. I know people. You made this guy's day. He probably acted like a model citizen for the rest of the week."

Shelia pushed her chair to the aisle, on the lookout for Angie. Shelia hadn't considered that part of her job might be to keep some pervert normal for a few hours. Granted it was a more important duty than registering dogs, but the slimy outside of it made it impossible for her to pick up and embrace. "I've got to go."

"Just because I told you something about yourself?"

"I'm not mad. There's no reason for me to get mad," but Shelia couldn't keep the strain from her voice.

"Wait, wait, what about the papers?"

"I can't get you papers, Todd; you have to get them from the former owner."

"She said the dog was purebred."

"I know it seems like it should be enough, but it's not."

"Like I give a shit about papers. I just thought if she had filed with you somewhere, I'd get them for her. She deserves it."

"She's a dog. She doesn't deserve anything."

"Hey, don't get mad. People get wrapped up in their animals. You should know that. Everybody needs somebody to love. You know that song?"

"I better go, then."

"Hey, don't go."

"I better. I'll get in trouble."

"I'll call you back tomorrow."

"Oh, you can't. The way they've got it set up is there's a whole room full of us taking calls, and we can't transfer a call on these phones. There's no guarantee you'd get me."

"That means you have to call me. Take down my number."

Shelia wrote Todd's number under her crude sketch.

"Don't leave just yet. Okay? I've got to answer the door."

Shelia listened to Todd and a man with a deeper voice. Shelia couldn't make out most of the conversation, but she heard enough to know the man's paycheck was late and he couldn't give Todd what he owed him. Shelia heard the man, then Todd laugh, like they both smelled the bullshit all over the story. She heard the shuffling and movement of bodies from one room to another. "Go get Samuel," Todd told the man, right before she heard voices from the television blare on. Shelia knew that you couldn't be choosy about people, that you might find a friend in an unlikely place, that many things can separate people, that it was wrong to judge. Still she couldn't shake the idea that calling long distance to an unmotivated drug dealer felt like a leap of good will or desperation that she couldn't justify.

"Sorry about that. You still there?" Todd said.

"I'm here."

"Did you hear he doesn't have my money?"

"Yeah, I heard. Listen, I better go. My manager's crazy. I might give you a call one day."

"You won't. I tell you I know people. That's okay." Todd covered the mouthpiece on his phone and said something to his visitor. Shelia thought she heard her name, but the word might have been she. "Did you say something?" Todd said to Shelia.

"No, I'm just waiting."

"Hey, I hope you'll call me, but if you can't, have a good life, okay?"

Shelia paused on the line, not sure she

wanted the call to end. "You too," Shelia said.

Shelia took a couple more calls as she blotted Todd's number out with her pen. The original digits became unrecognizable in a nest of squiggles and circles.

By the time Shelia got to the bathroom, Wendy was already there, combing and smoothing down her hair into a bob.

"One second," Shelia dashed into the nearest stall. She hated for anyone to hear her pee, but only so many times you can flush the toilet and not seem obsessive.

Wendy wore her pancake makeup thick as icing on her face and neck, long-sleeved dresses or turtlenecks and tea-length skirts every day, though she wasn't in the least bit religious like the girls Shelia knew from home, with only their shins exposed, their flat feet in unfashionable shoes, faces young looking and unadorned. Wendy never mentioned God, didn't pray over her homemade sandwich, never said the first word of conversion to a single soul. But once they all noticed the bruises on her arms and legs, there was no need at all to ask why about the dresses. Still Shelia was annoyed by Wendy. You'd think that someone in her difficult and embarrassing situation would try to blend in, but not Wendy. At every turn, she'd be laughing too loud or telling some story where she was always right. A lot of people noticed, if the hard looks and rolled eyes at Wendy were any indication. But once they saw the bruises, nobody said a thing to her. The beatings she was taking from somebody, probably her boyfriend, were enough for her to deal with in one lifetime.

The other two women in their training class were old enough to be mothers to Wendy and Shelia. Jenny was fifty-five if she was a day and had eliminated herself from the friend race when she told them all how she once had the best sex of her life on the hood of a stranger's pickup. Dot, the black woman in her late forties, had never married, had no children, and still lived with her mother but was ruled out because she couldn't forget that day at the TWA counter, a suited bigwig handed her and all her friends pink slips declaring, "The airline's bankrupt, forget your pension and don't come back." Shelia thought that some things you got to let scurry under the rock where you found them. But Dot believed she had let go, cut with bolt cutters the last ties that kept her to that biggest rejection and heartbreak. The problem was the rejection stuck to her like a Siamese twin. After a half-dozen times of the same pitiful story with the same pitiful pauses, people learned to see Dot and walk the other way.

Forget about the other employees; they had their own friends from their own training classes. Friends that they guarded like gold bullion. Shelia thought she hadn't really made a friend in years, though she craved the connection. Just a few nights like the night outside her grandmother's as a child, bats circling a lofted basketball high in the air almost all the way to the dirt when the circle of them swooped back up just in time to miss the smack of the ground. Shelia would stand outside with her cousins and listen to the sound of the crenellated wings, flapping like crazy, making her ache with fear. But this moment she remembered with happiness. She and her cousins and neighborhood friends screaming at the bats loud and together in the night.

"Hurry up, I've got to show you something," Wendy said.

As soon as Shelia opened the stall door, Wendy had her hand out displaying a ring shaped like an amoeba with dirty-looking chips of diamonds or glass in a shiny setting.

"Wow," Shelia said, but she meant *why* and reached out to touch Wendy's hand.

"Wash your hands, girl," Wendy snatched her hand back.

"That's pretty," Shelia said, concentrating on the lather on her hands so she didn't have to see Wendy's reflection in the restroom mirror. "Sorry it took me a minute, I had a long call."

"Can you believe it?" Wendy said admiring her ring. "It's not a usual shape."

Shelia glanced at her own ring, a small quarter-carat stone, milky now from soap and lotion buildup. Not big, but real, she'd helped pick it out not yet a year ago. She could have done without one and would have if Polo hadn't insisted. He was a good man overall. They'd moved from their hometown, and now Polo was in college getting a degree in business. Who cared if he sat and talked with his friends, a lot of them women, laughing like fools about things Shelia couldn't know about and that never translated when they tried to explain, "Oh, you had to be there," they'd hoot. But she was there. Standing right there. Shelia would work full-time now, but soon, it would be her turn. Soon, when Polo graduated, when Polo found a job, when Polo got established just a little, Shelia would get everything she wanted. And she believed it mostly. Except for the evenings at the tiny apartment, the unmade, fold-out couch for a bed, no cute bric-a-brac or books cocked just so on top of polished wood, no smiling faces from honeymoon pictures or matching china, but more layers of mess. Each room more junked than the last. Clothes, shoes, and the bags from the fast food they lived on strewn in every direction. *We're busy,* Shelia tried to tell herself so she wouldn't think that she was living her real life, just rehearsing. But she could hold out. Forget the picture of her second day of work, tears running in rivulets down her face, no sobbing, not at all, but tears coming with a force she couldn't control. She told Betsy and the others in the training group that she had terrible allergies, "This happens every once in a while," she'd said.

"But Shelia," Betsy'd said, "your eyes are clear as day."

"Darryl told me he had me a surprise, but I never expected this."

"It's nice," Shelia said.

"I needed to tell you that we are going away this weekend so we can't come over." Shelia worked with Wendy for eight months, and she'd never seen Darryl except from a distance from the car when he came to pick Wendy up in the afternoons. He was shy or tired or sick or leaving town or just coming back into town, months' worth of reasons why they could never get together or why Wendy could not leave the house by herself. Shelia'd planned to clean the apartment, really clean, set a table, eat a meal like grown-ups, like nice people are supposed to do. The knowledge that now there was no reason to do that made Shelia unsteady on her feet.

Wendy's pancake makeup was smeared on the bodice of her dress, all over the sleeves, but she seemed not to see it and concentrated on her hair.

"You been in here long?" Shelia managed.

"A couple minutes," Wendy sighed, giving up on more compliments on the ring. "Do you like my hair better like this or with the bangs?"

There was no right answer. Her bangs rarely sat on her forehead and were as flat and unmanageable as cardboard, but on the other hand, the bob looked lacquered like an ear flap hat. She had ugly hair made uglier by the helmet styles she chose. Shelia wondered if she was thinking like a white person. All her life she had heard people tell other black people that they were acting white or thinking white — some had even said it about her. Shelia had always dismissed the idea as a phoney, convenient insult to hurl because it couldn't be defended. It had not occurred to Shelia until now that a part of it might be true.

"Either way," Shelia said and avoided Wendy's eyes and smoothed her own hair back into a ponytail.

"Don't clown me. Answer."

"I'm not playing with you," Shelia said and tried not to sound annoyed. "The bangs, I guess." Wendy combed bangs across her forehead into a large curl while Shelia watched. The two of them had minutes together at most. There was no time to waste.

"Do you remember Bathsheba from the Bible?" Shelia asked.

"Bathsheba? Wasn't she the one who turned into salt?"

"No, I don't think so."

"That was her. God told her not to turn around, but she did and turned into a pillar of salt. That's a screwed-up story."

"No, that wasn't Bathsheba," Shelia said louder than she meant to.

"You're in a mood, aren't you?" Wendy began. "Angie get on your nerves?"

"I'm used to her," Shelia said, though she wasn't and never would be. Shelia had never before been yelled at like a trained animal.

She hated Wendy for reminding her of the moment.

"Well, you'll get a better ring. It took Darryl two years to come up with this one," Wendy smiled, looking at her new ring.

Shelia glanced at herself in the mirror. There are few moments of cold, clear-eyed intelligence in life. Moments you will not have to return to, to reconstruct, to examine or dissect for motivation or meaning, uncomplicated by trauma or love or savage indifference. Shelia felt this moment acutely like the first merciless dive into cold water. Years later, the feeling would return to her with clarity and pain like a slap, making her sick with her own cruel impulses.

"What's on your arm?" Shelia said in almost a whisper, pointing to Wendy's wrist.

"Makeup," Wendy quickly shifted her cuff down to cover her wrist. She wet a towel and began grinding her thick brown foundation into the fabric.

"No, Wendy," Shelia began, her voice cracked. "I saw something," Shelia stared at Wendy in the mirror.

Wendy tried to adjust her dress and sleeves, not sure whether she could trust that Shelia had seen nothing.

"Makeup, I said," Wendy snapped and looked at Shelia's eyes in the mirror. Shelia would have to wrestle Wendy to the ground to see her naked arm.

Shelia saw herself yank up Wendy's sleeve. She could imagine the red and purple marks in various stages of healing, multicolored swirls like a van Gogh sky, all over Wendy's body. When they both saw it, they could stare it down and call it what it was. But Shelia knew she wouldn't wrestle Wendy for a truth neither of them wanted.

"Maybe I'm wrong," Shelia said and wanted to take back her delight in Wendy's pain. That wasn't who she was at all, not at the bone. "I like your ring, really," but the incredulity of how anyone could go to a jewelry store or pawn shop and choose that ugly little reminder of love's acceptances was all over Shelia's face.

"You got here so late, we don't have any time left." Wendy moved toward the door, her eyes downcast. Wendy was angry, but she would recover. There was nobody out there she could talk to either.

Shelia waited behind the closed door to give Wendy a few seconds' head start back to their phone stations. Shelia felt tiny and bitter like early fruit. But she tried to think of the happy days she rode with her mother to pick up her daddy at Plant 3. She loved to hear the whistle that marked the end of the shift, mostly because only seconds later her father and his friends, all young men then, in their twenties and thirties, but even some of the old-timers, streamed through the double doors of the furniture factory, running like the place was on fire, running to their rides and their waiting wives and girlfriends, relief and sawdust on their faces. Shelia loved the flood of the men spreading out in all directions except back inside. Few things had been better than the breathless moment when she picked out her father from the group, the seconds she waited all day for, this uncomplicated joy. But no vision would come.

Shelia counted to five and opened the door to the ladies' room. Just over an hour and a half to go. She could do that on her head. Of course she could pick up her bag, her book, and walk the couple of miles to her apartment. Start over in some lesser-known place. Nothing kept her tethered and trapped like a yard dog on a short chain. But unless you are there and have lived it, don't you dare talk about how the door both opens and closes. Or how it is as simple to find the way to someplace else as it is to walk the few carpeted steps back to the cubicle, back to the headphones and the next caller in the queue.

As usual, we weren't exactly doing what you might call good business at Holly Acres, and as usual, I was slouched in the doorway on the phone with Maggie Rogers. I knew that I should make some Jehovah's Witness friends and I wanted to, but Maggie and I clicked. We'd park and watch from lookouts on Brushy Mountain Road the few twinkles of amber light in our tiny town below. We had the same sense of humor and the same inability to appreciate our peers. When Wendy Jenkins jazz-danced at our school assembly to "The Entertainer," Maggie said that was all she ever needed to know of hell. Still I knew that one day, we would have to part the ways, me as a real Jehovah's Witness with only Jehovah's Witness friends and she with her own friends in college or miles away in one of the cities she'd lived in when her dad was in what their family called his *uncertain phase.* For now, I needed someone to talk to and talk as long as I pleased. In a few minutes, Matt's chubby girlfriend with the black mane of hair she touched to make sure you noticed it, would show up and hijack him to her mother's Impala. Tim, the cook, was already smoking whatever he had handy behind the Dumpsters. Without Maggie, I'd just be standing around here alone, waiting for the imaginary rush of customers with their stock-exchange money raised in the air walking out with brightly colored boxes of chicken like department-store gifts.

"Damn, there's the whore," Matt yelled. I'd learned to ignore him, and I would have then if I hadn't been supposed to work the cash register. If I had a dollar for every girl he called a whore, a dyke, a loser, a bitch, I'd quit this job and watch television reruns like any self-respecting teenager in the 1980s. Matt spotted a good-looking woman, knew he was minutes from rejection, and lashed out first. But Shelby was a working girl, so they said, the real deal waltzing into Holly Acres chicken like anybody else.

"I gotta go," I whispered into the receiver, not waiting for Maggie to reply. I'd call her later. We talked mornings on the way to school, every day in our classes, evenings while I worked, and at night after my shift was over. Tonight I would actually have something to tell her.

"Somebody's going to hear you one of these days," I said, glaring in Matt's direction.

"I want them to hear. Hell, people need a little bit of truth," he chuckled, looking around for Tim to hyena-laugh with him. I rolled my eyes. Matt would die standing there, if anyone dared share any real truth about him.

By the time I got behind my register, Shelby was already in the restaurant hunched into the refrigerator like if she searched hard enough she might find buried treasure, her shorts inched up on her legs revealing the soft W of her bare behind. Shelby didn't look at me or at Matt but held to the light, like a jeweler, a couple of the see-through containers of mashed-potato salad and a few sad desserts. Kentucky Fried Chicken had the monopoly on takeout chicken in our town, and our particular tastes just couldn't compete. Besides, our stuff wasn't very good. Shelby placed a container of slaw on the counter. I should've warned her. Our trash was full of untouched, unexpired slaw. The nicest thing we heard from customers about it was it had a "funny taste." Shelby stretched, lifted her skinny arms above her head, the expanse of exposed white belly growing before our eyes. She could have been a porn star or in a better world the most popular girl at Central High.

"Hey, Shelby," Matt crooned, managing to sound both nasty and stupid.

"Hey there," Shelby said. If I didn't already know Matt, I would have thought she was glad to see him.

"Well, who are you?" Shelby teased, leaned in my direction against the counter. She was just tall enough that her boobs had a convenient shelf.

"I'm fine," I said, though I quickly realized that I'd answered the wrong question.

She was pretty close up, not a porn-star hard face at all, but delicate with a twitching bunny mouth. I'm not sure what I was expecting, maybe some reptile deadness in the eyes, maybe a world-weary sigh at every mundane little thing. I don't know, but she surprised me. If this were a bad movie, I would have rubbed both eyes with my fists not sure of what I was seeing.

"Are you new?" Shelby's accent was thick, a farmer's daughter from the tired jokes.

"Not really," I said. I'd been working for two years. Nearly every shift, sometimes as much as a full-time job during the week, but I'd never seen Shelby in the restaurant or anywhere else in town. But no way you could spend much time in Carboro without hearing about her. I'd wanted to get a good look at the woman who did that. In our small Southern town not much stayed secret. The latest rumor was that Jamie Johnson, the blackest boy in school, had tried to pick Shelby up at Margie's, the black nightclub in town. Shelby, perched on a bar stool like a little white bird, her blonde hair crested and fluffed, most of her pale legs exposed like she was comfortable, like she belonged there. Jamie bought her a drink, while the other men waved encouragement. I'm sure they must have thought it hilarious that this black ugly boy thought somebody was interested. How embarrassed he'd been to find out she wasn't for real and that nothing she said or did could be trusted.

"Baby drumsticks, honey, with a little cup of barbeque sauce, okay?" Shelby said.

I was about to call the order over my shoulder but Matt must have gone to get Tim, and both of them were standing there looking dumber than usual. I could only see them from the waist up, the top halves of their bodies in the opening where we put the orders, looking like redneck puppet theater. They were fine, good boys, I guess. If you ignore that they turned anything into sex. Don't get them started about the size and heft of the taters, the ooze of dish-washing liquid into the larger-than-life tubs they washed the trays in. I laughed at them at first, in the girl way, *Stop it, ya'll are so gross.* But it got old fast. About the ninth time I saw Matt put chicken breasts on his own flat chest, prance and mince around the cooking area, it just wasn't funny anymore.

Matt fumbled in the chicken warmer for the drumsticks. The crinkle of the stiff paper we used to catch most of the grease underneath sounded like he was fumbling for Valentine candy. He grabbed a few baby drums, shook the large metal tater tray, shifting the fried taters side-to-side, shaking up the potatoes to keep the flour from sticking under the hot warmer light, in a way I'm sure he thought manly. Usually Matt would hand me the orders, but there he came, rounding the corner to the front counter, without his paper hat.

"This is for you, baby," Matt held onto the box but inched it closer and closer to Shelby across the counter.

She didn't reach out to take it but watched Matt's face, her expression flat, her eyes clear and unblinking.

"I'm playing with you, baby," Matt said as he sent the box toward her chest like he'd loosed a wind-up car. "Here then," Matt waited, hoping Shelby would say she was sorry, that he was hilarious after all.

"Thank you, honey," Shelby smiled at me. "I'm going to eat it here."

Shelby took the first booth in the dining room, the only table I could see from behind the counter. She twisted one leg under the other on the cheap pressed-wood bench and spread her paper napkin in her lap picnic style.

It was as good a time as any to wipe down the tables in the narrow dining room. I grabbed the lump of soapy rag we kept on the shelf under the cash register and tried not to meet Shelby's eyes. The cheap industrial carpet in front of the bathroom doors had worn thin, making the floor look dirty no matter how many times we vacuumed. Nobody cared. We all understood that this job wouldn't last, that one day in the not-so-distant future we would pass by this very building, that would then be a Tantastic or Yount Insurance, without even a flutter of recognition. The only real believer was our fool manager: "If you have time to lean, you have time to clean," she'd snarl, if she saw you idle. Too many times I had to clean the tater-prep area, my ragged finger in the slimy joints and crevices of the two-tiered pan. Or worse, I had to scrub the wire chicken racks the boys dunked into the washing-machine-sized fryers, my brush grazing the surface, crusted grease and skin flying upward like welder's fire.

I wiped the tables and seats down my side to Shelby so I could see if she made motions to leave.

"You go to West Wilkes?" Shelby said.

I nodded to her.

"That's good, you should stay in school," Shelby ate her chicken wings like a rabbit, with the tips of the fingers on both hands.

"Where did you go? To school, I mean," I said, wrapping the rag around my hand like a boxer.

"Who cares," Shelby smiled between chews. "All I know is I'm getting the hell out of this town. I can tell you that much," Shelby said. "I'm thinking Florida. Someplace warm. Never been there though," Shelby stopped and gestured with her chicken wing. "I did go to Georgia when I was five with my daddy and his sister. Most of it I don't remember."

"I've got a cousin in Atlanta, but she hates

it," I said. I couldn't think of anything else to add. I'd never been anywhere either.

What was I thinking? The restaurant was a fishbowl full of floor-to-ceiling windows. Just beyond the parking lot Highway 18 looked like a runway, a straight shot, launching me anywhere, or so I thought, until my eyes settled on the across-the-street hamburger joint and throngs of my classmates in bunches spilling out of cars like adolescent clowns, making me forget that I was in the middle of my life, in the eye of it, and forcing me to see myself from the outside. I didn't like the view. Besides, I was a Jehovah's Witness. A *Jehovah's Witness* for God's sake. I wouldn't and couldn't go to a birthday party or smoke a cigarette. I knocked on people's doors on weekends, on weekdays after school, or when I wasn't working. I was supposed to introduce myself as a Jehovah's Witness within thirty seconds of meeting someone — not a rule, but a protection. You'd be amazed at the people you could clear out of your path, stop in their friendly, lecherous, or people-interested tracks with those words.

"I bet you eat here every night, don't you?"

"I used to. You get sick of it quicker than you think. They won't let me in the house if

I have a chicken box."

Shelby laughed. "Sounds like ya'll have fun."

I hadn't thought about what we did as fun. After my shift I'd wait to eat with my brothers and mother. They'd pick me up from work, my little brother quiet and sometimes half-asleep, and the four of us would sit in front of the television, my brother's head stuck into the brown and orange chicken bucket searching for thighs, all of our faces greasy and content flickering from the light of the television. I never thought about it as fun.

Matt and Tim paused from behind the counter, listening. We couldn't see them, but their fool-laughing broke through to the dining room every few minutes. They were talking about us.

"Customer," Matt yelled.

"You take this one, Matt," I yelled.

"What," he flung open the door into the dining room, pretending to be annoyed so we wouldn't suspect that all he'd wanted was some reason to join us.

"Nothing," I said, waving him off. "Nothing. I forgot."

"Ya'll don't have many customers, do you? I guess that's good for you, right?" Shelby was giving me permission to get up. I was surprised that I cared, like I was on a date that despite all indications was going well.

"I'll be back," I said, the closest I could come to asking her to stay. I didn't want to say that I wished we had so many people that I could take the orders, pour the fountain drinks, make change so fast that I could do it in my sleep. I wanted so many people in the store that nobody stood out and every face was a blur through the door.

A youngish couple waited in their low-riding car, not talking, waiting, like they expected me to come rolling out on skates. A toddler with thin brown hair to her narrow shoulders, pressed her cheek pressed like a cool comfort on the back window.

"Should we get the Holly special?" the man said to the girl, jiggling her on his arm, his fat moustache an inch from her forehead. The child said nothing, picked at the dirty knees on her tights.

"Get what you want," the woman answered, resting her back on the large plate-glass window. The man looked at me and winked like we both hated the woman he was with together.

"The Holly's going to be fifteen, twenty minutes," Matt yelled to the couple hoping to discourage them so he wouldn't have to cook.

"We can wait," the man said, setting the little girl down.

"They haven't found those boys in Miller's Creek," the woman said to me. "They said it on the radio, just right now."

Everybody speculated about what could have happened. We'd all seen in the newspaper and on television the sweet department-store picture of the little boys dressed like tiny hunters in matching-plaid shirts, overlapping each other like pups.

"I know for a fact a cult got them," the man said.

"You don't know what the hell you're talking about," the woman said.

The man leaned onto the counter. "In Love Valley, they do things like that. You don't know what some people can do. I used to live down there, I know."

The woman sucked her lip in disgust. "What does a cult want with little boys?" she laughed.

"You name it."

The little girl had inched herself away from her parents almost to the booth where Shelby sat. Shelby must have looked to her like a wonder, too.

"Tabitha, get over here, leave people

alone," the woman yelped.

"Aren't you a sweet doll baby?" Shelby leaned down to her, laughed in the direction of the couple to make sure they knew she meant no harm.

"Order." Matt yelled like I wouldn't notice the big bucket of chicken in the window. That, probably more than anything, made me give them their big bucket free.

"You sure?" the man said, like he expected a trick.

I tried not to look weary. Goodness knows I did, but a body gets tired of offering the remedy nobody wants.

"You see that, Carol," the man glared at the woman, like he'd won a contest, beating her at a game she thought she had down cold. The woman rolled her eyes, already halfway out the door.

"Give the nice girl a kiss," the man instructed the child; dangling her from her waist, her face raised to my height, so if I leaned across I could reach her round cheek over the counter.

The little girl's expression didn't change as she rested her hands on my face and jammed her tiny tongue in my mouth.

"Good girl," the man hoisted her up to his chest. "Now, say thank you."

I tried to find Shelby then, anybody who could tell me what I knew for sure, but Shelby'd turned away.

"Thank you," the child whispered into the air between me and the door.

Shelby cleaned the table with the flat of her hand, wiped her face with a moist towelette. She looked like she was leaving.

"I hate it here," and as soon as I said it, the bold truth of it scared me.

"You can get another job," Shelby said, but she knew I didn't mean the job. Shelby sucked from her straw and cast her eyes down to the top of her cup.

"I had a job in a barbeque place in Elkin. My brother got it for me. I wasn't but fourteen but the owner, we called him Big Nasty, would let me work for cash. He was crazy. He wanted us to rinse out the paper cups people didn't take with them," Shelby raised her eyebrows in disbelief. "I was a kid, but I knew that wasn't sanitary, you know?" I nodded, waiting for Shelby to tell the rest of the story.

"What did you do?"

"I did what he said. I would have rinsed out soda cans, if he asked. He was the one with the cash."

I laughed but didn't see anything funny.

255

"I'll get you some more," I reached for her soda.

"Yeah, I'll take one for the road."

Shelby followed me to the counter while I jangled the crushed ice into the cup, the soda foaming over the top.

"You've got pretty eyes," Shelby said. "You do," she insisted like I'd disagreed. "There are all kinds of pretty outside of Wilkes County," she said.

I knew my face was too thin and pointed. I'd been called Hatchet enough times to know I had a nose too big. It would be years before I believed in pretty. "I'm a Jehovah's Witness," I blurted.

Shelby nodded like I'd revealed something obvious.

"I thought ya'll couldn't wear pants," she said.

"No, that's Holiness people. We're the ones that come to your door."

"Yeah, I know," she jabbed in the straw, dragged, found nothing but air between the chips of ice, the desperate sucking sounds making me so sad I thought I might cry.

"I thought there was more in there than that," I said as I reached for her cup.

"Get used to it," Shelby said, and this time we both laughed for real.

Shelby took the newly filled soda, bowed

the straw up and down in the cup, the motion sounding like she was tuning a violin.

"You're a Jehovah's Witness. That's a good thing to be, right?" she said, her face looking sincere.

The last time I remember hearing Shelby's name was a shock. I'd been waiting for my ride on the deck of our big two-story rental house, an old house, but solid with plenty of rooms. The owner liked my mother. Actually, he didn't really know her. Better said, he felt sorry for her. She was a pretty, young woman trying to have a decent life with her kids and no man. He thought the least he could do was to let her have the old place for cheap. And it was a good place. We had a large wooden deck, and though I knew it impossible, I saw it dressed up in lights and teak furniture, mounds of food and colorful, umbrellaed drinks circulating in the hands and on the plates of our guests. We had an upstairs with large bedrooms and a strange little room with a sloped ceiling. Who cared that summer's wall of heat kept us sequestered on the ground floor, sweaty piles of bodies positioned in front of two ancient electric fans? Move-in day we hesitated in each room, peered around corners tentatively like we were expecting a jack-in-the-box to pop out of every closet and around each wall or we were in a good dream that, if we were quiet enough, didn't have to end. Before the road came through, this must have been a place for middle-class people. The only drawback was that only ten feet of yard and a narrow porch separated us from the busy highway. And even in the dead of night, we could hear the whir of cars rushing to the outskirts of town, to what passed as suburbs. What a pity that now no one would ever buy all this space and good light.

Linda was going to drive up any minute, and I wanted to be ready. It wasn't enough to sit in the kitchen and listen for the crunch of gravel of her car in the driveway. I wanted to be on the deck eager and ready the second she came. I hoped she was alone. Her older girl was fine, sweet, a chubby kid with good home training and a lot of well-rehearsed answers. But the twins I avoided. They watched me like baby dictators or old men in a candy store, like I might run out with a jawbreaker. They didn't get that from Linda. She approached the whole wide world like she was opening a jewel box, nothing closed and remote, and any little bauble she desired, she could pinch her fingers into the velvet and wear it to bed, if she wanted. I tried to explain her to my grandmother. "Linda Cashion is happy all the time. For real," I told my grandmother. "She let her four-year-old kick the back of her car seat over and over. While she was driving," I insisted. "Know what she did then? She laughed and sang to him, 'I feel a little foot in my back' like 'Pop Goes the Weasel.' What does it all mean?" I pleaded. I wanted my grandmother to tell me Linda's secret to life, unravel the threads of it, so I could see it in its pure form, memorize it, have it, too. "It means she ain't no black woman with real problems," my grandmother said.

Linda picked her light brown curls straight up at every light to make sure that the thinnest part of her Afro looked like a halo in the fading light. Linda is white. White as they come. But she preferred the soul-sister do or maybe better described as the Annie Redux Early Middle Age style. I imagined how it happens. One day you need milk from the grocery store or eggs, some staple or final ingredient, the thing you can't do without, and there you are: sweat pants, hair in some configuration, your face ashen and nude. But one day the thought, just an itch at first, but the thought emerges, who will see? If the answer is *nobody,* then it has begun. You blend into the stand of tomatoes, mounds of cantaloupes, row of green beans in a chaotic heap. And so what if the public sees, none of them look one bit better, and you stumble onto a truth you are startled that you couldn't have figured out before: all that time, those years of fussing and primping in the mirror only to discover that there is no penalty for *matronly.* Part of Linda's charm was that she reveled in the just-as-you-are.

"Sarah-Donna is doing so well. I want her to start coming to the meetings. Making the Truth her own," Linda said. "She is missing so much," Linda sighed into the mirror. "At least she's getting to meet you. She needs a good friend, a Proverbs 18:24."

I had my first weekday off from work in a long time, and I had a date with two hours of after-school rerun television. My favorite was *What's Happening.* Here's the premise: a single, black, kind, smart, hugely fat mother who works as a maid has a teenage son and daughter who stay home alone for several hours after they get home from school. The show focuses on the unstructured time the kids have with each other and with friends while Mom is working. Every episode without fail the mother grabs

260

her bone-skinny son in a thick embrace, squeezing him from love or pride or consolation, causing the young man to exclaim, "Mama, I can't breathe." Hilarious. I anticipated the line but never saw it coming. *What's Happening* was as good as it sounds.

Still I wanted to impress Linda. She was married to a Cashion, a member of one of the well-to-do families in town. It was always a coup to get a local believer into our congregation of Jehovah's Witnesses, but a rich, respected local was even better. Linda left a comfortable family to be with us; nice people who carol at Christmas for fun; decorous people who hid their dirt under years of silence and repression like God intended. When these folks got together, I bet money that no one showed up at the end of the party, like my Uncle Alvin, loose from a few bottles of whatever he could find, sloshing from family member to family member, eighty-proof breath in our faces, "Do you love me? I need to know. Do you?" If someone like her could turn her back on a smooth, happy life to run around door-to-door, what was my excuse? So when Linda called, I put on my least-wrinkled circle skirt, wrestled my hair back in a severe bun, what I like to call my hair's missionary position, and gathered my Bible, tracts, and the Paradise book.

Linda and I got to her Bible study's white wooden frame house. The porch was hardly big enough for both of us to stand at a comfortable distance. I rested my arm on the porch railing, and bits of peeling paint adhered to my blouse. I resisted the impulse to peel some of it off. I didn't want Linda to think I was too wrapped up in my appearance.

"Come in," a woman's voice rang out at us. "Door's open."

The woman stood with her back to us, her hands in sudsy dishwater.

"Hey, Linda. Ya'll have a seat," she called over her back, "I'm just going to dry my hands."

I liked the cozy rooms, the kitchen and living room open to each other, every inch of space covered and decorated. I've always liked the feel of houses that seem collated together, the decorator's spirits undaunted by the lack of money, each couch, figurine, side table dragged in and married to other found items. The woman motioned for us sit. She was twenty-five, if she was a day, but from a distance she could pass for my age. Sarah-Donna sat herself on the longest couch, which faced the oversized love seat where Linda and I sat. Sarah-Donna was plain and gangly, her long legs crossing and uncrossing, like she was nervous and couldn't figure out what to do with herself. Linda told me that Sarah-Donna reminded her of a woman who walked right past her and into her house in California, made herself a peanut butter sandwich, and walked out without a word.

"Mama's coming back soon. I told her ya'll would be here," Sarah-Donna said. "She won't mind ya'll coming. She just don't want to hear none of it herself." Sarah-Donna smiled.

"We'll be as quick as we can," Linda said, ignoring the Jew reference, but I could see her storing away the phrase for a future lesson.

I was glad to hear we wouldn't stay. I hated the idea of the mother coming in, her jaw dropping, her muttering to herself, or worse, passing right by us without a word.

"Before we start, can I ask you something?" Sarah-Donna said.

"Of course," Linda closed her book and put it between us on the sofa, letting Sarah-Donna see she wasn't a bit worried about getting on with the lesson.

"Did you hear about Shelby?" Sarah-Donna began. "So sad. Well, I didn't hear it, but plenty of other people did. Sad."

For months I'd wanted someone to say Shelby's name out loud, to hear the sound of it, hear about her, to feel the relief from the necessity, the load of having her on my mind. Linda didn't like gossip and looked a little scared that she was about to open a snake-charmer's basket. If there existed a way to shift the conversation, she'd find it. Stick to the positive, talk about our future plans, about Bible study, about working more in the field service, about maybe becoming a missionary in some backward country without television, Jordache, or Top 40. She would never have wanted to talk to us about Shelby, but Sarah-Donna was determined.

"Ya'll did hear, right?" Sarah-Donna pressed.

"No. What happened to her? Is she all right?" Linda said.

"She's got The AIDS."

"Oh dear," Linda said.

AIDS talk was everywhere. For all I know, AIDS was the first disease that the public saw doctors wrestle with, refine their assessments. It's no wonder that we imagined the worst. Now, no matter what anyone said, we knew that anybody could get The AIDS any time. Sex? Needles? A yodel or drawn-out stare? Yes, yes, and needs more research.

"They announced it yesterday on WKBC. They said everybody had to stay away from her. The danger, you know it? You never think something like that is going to happen around here," Sarah-Donna shook her head, but I could tell she was excited.

It was a good story. The town prostitute, the worst sinner, gets the worst disease we know.

"The Bible says all about that, right? Eye for an eye, right? I mean you have to pay for your sins," Sarah-Donna said.

"They will receive recompense in their own flesh," Linda said as she held her Bible like a shield.

Shelby's body fooled her, but that could happen to anybody. Before you know it, you are led to places you can't begin to understand. I've felt it. There have been days when I thought if only I'd had someone to touch me, make the ache I couldn't name stop, tell me the pain I held in my lockbox of a heart was useful, a necessary thing to finally usher me into a kind of paradise I could get to from here. Of course, that was wrong. The trick you learn, after years, sometimes, is that pain is just pain.

I couldn't help but chuckle. Linda smiled in my direction, assuming she'd be let in on the joke at any minute. "They called her a

265

whore," I said. That's not what I wanted to say, but killing Shelby made me strong.

Linda's eyes flapped open at *whore*.

"They should call her what she is. Everybody knows it," I said, my voice sounded crusted.

"Well, she can serve as an example for all of us," Linda began. She riffled through her bag, trying to divert my attention. "Okay, let's go ahead and get started."

"What I was asking is, will she go to hell? You know like Hitler, like that?" Sarah-Donna worried the threads dangling from her cutoff jeans.

"Yeah, maybe she can die, and we can all learn something," I said. "That would be good."

Linda winced to Sarah-Donna who looked from my face to Linda's not sure what to think.

"No, no," Linda said, as calm as ever, but I could hear the gathering of forces in her voice. "Remember what we said about the condition of the dead, about hell and hellfire? Besides, any of us can turn our lives around at any time . . ."

"I heard it on the radio," I said. Though I hadn't heard a word. Linda hadn't looked at me straight on yet, but now she twisted in her seat to face me.

"You heard it?" Linda said. "Are you sure?" Linda said willing me to recant, daring me to say I'd heard about Shelby from a friend of a friend, in a checkout line, maybe she even hoped I would.

"I heard it," I said.

"Well," she sighed in a kind of conclusion, "that's enough about such a terrible thing."

"Yeah. She's gone now, that's enough," I pulled out the study book from my scuffed-up bag and flipped loudly through the pages. Somehow, I kept coming back to the happy pictures of a clean new world, its edges rounded and safe.

"She's got people in Florida," I said. "But she's gone now. Long gone from here," my voice cracked but I kept going, "She can ruin somebody else's neighborhood now."

"This talk isn't useful," Linda snapped. "We don't learn anything, and we are here to learn and teach," Linda's book slid off her lap onto the hardwood floor. She smiled at Sarah-Donna. "We don't have much time."

Sarah-Donna read each of the paragraphs, and Linda asked her questions printed on the bottom of every page. The three of us were on the same latitude and longitude, in the same rickety little house, even reading the same words, but I was breathing different air.

I wouldn't be Linda's friend. Never. But at least in that moment, I didn't need it. It was liberating to walk away from the burning building, the stink of charred wood behind you. That the good feeling doesn't last is tragic and obvious.

After a few months, I stopped waiting for Shelby. She said she'd come back to the restaurant to talk sometime — no date — just some time. She had asked me to visit her, preaching or not, but she didn't give me an address; only a direction. I'd spent a lot of energy trying to figure her out, but mostly I daydreamed about her, imagining us together: getting ready in the bathroom, me burning my eyeliner pencil to rim my eyes with the thickest black line like Cleopatra. Shelby on the toilet, her bony knees pressed together, panties puddled between her feet, laughing and talking over the trickle of piss. I had no idea, not even any imagination what might happen next or where we might go or what people did in their remote ordinary lives or how anyone ever made it through or out and over or ever got anywhere intact or even alive without huddling for fear, sick and disgusted with the desire of the world, but paralyzed about what to do. Neither of us would know how to act with the well-adjusted, but for a long time, it was enough to replay in a loop the dream of our sparkling entrance, watch us strutting in once, thirty, a thousand times. Though I told no one, I was embarrassed that Shelby was so important to me. And lately, when I catch myself thinking about her, wishing for her to appear, I am just ashamed. The same vile feeling as if someone smacked a nasty word in my direction that I pretended I didn't hear.

THERE CAN NEVER BE ANOTHER ME

Mae and Jonnie called their place *Sisters*. The name sounded good, but they were actually mother and daughter, separated by little more than twenty years, but mother and daughter nonetheless. Sisters wasn't a fine dining place, just a tiny room in the front of an old house on Damascus Church Road, with three lightweight dirty tables and chairs bought for a couple of dollars from the recently closed-up Chinese place, aptly named *House of Chow*. Mae and Jonnie covered the uncleanable tabletops with plastic cloths, set salt and pepper shakers and hot sauce in the middle of each like a bouquet. At first, Mae kept napkins on the tables, but customers would use them like they were the last paper products on earth. Take five when the corner of one would have done fine. Use them to wipe fingers, noses, the tips of shoes, eyes, clean underarms, and save for panty liners. When they were sitting out like that, who wouldn't assume that there was always more? Sisters wasn't decorated except for a yard-sale clock, but neither woman cared too much for fussing over things, creating some kind of room with the books just so, the pillows fluffed, no shoes or spilled toys to spoil the scene. Neither cared for the fantasy decorating encouraged. Besides, Sisters was not the establishment to go to if you are looking for scenery, garnishes, or flourishes to please the eye, food piled in artful stacks, or for watching fancy people. The mission at Sisters is to get all you want to eat and go home full. That's enough entertainment for anybody.

Mae was good-looking for a woman her age. That's what people always added, *a woman her age.* She was skinny but carried herself like a big woman with her arms out to her sides like parentheses, always straightening her top over her hips like she had something to hide, smoothing her clothes from the creases her imaginary rolls of fat made, habits probably picked up from years of watching her large mother negotiate the world. Mae would have been pretty except for her black-rimmed lips that she tried to hide except when a big laugh made her forget. When she was a little younger the rumor was she'd open her legs for anybody, though like most things, it wasn't all-the-way true. She'd been fooled a few times, standing and lying, small and lonesome because somebody said on Saturday night that he'd be around on Monday, but who hasn't felt some of that?

If Don had been looking for a woman at all, his first glance would have lighted on Mae. She was close to his age, and he'd known her all his life. At one time, that familiarity would have repelled Don. He wasn't sure when it became a plus, when the unknown and exotic lost their appeal. Don even liked the weave that stretched Mae's neat little Afro to silky black hair beyond Mae's shoulders. Hair everybody in town knew had recently belonged to some Korean woman. Hair that everyone knew stood in for the hair Mae pulled out herself the second she discovered her beloved mother would never wake up from her last dream.

At the funeral, Mae didn't even bother to hide the bald patch but let the world see on her own body a piece of what had happened to her heart. At the end of the service, as she tried to pass by the coffin the pallbearers set up at the door, Mae saw her lying like she had all the time in the world, patiently, like she never was in her real life, and Mae couldn't stop screaming, for minutes that seemed like hours that had everyone teary in the middle of their own private losses. Mae's daughter, Reverend Johnson, her boyfriend, everybody tried to tell her different, but she knew that life would forever pale, the luster flaked away like leaded paint. People felt sorry, but they talked about it, saying things like she didn't need to do all that, and she should have tried to get hold of herself for the children present, but Don admired her for it. When else do you get to rail and plead with God, beg him for a last chance, another day? When his time came, Don used to want none of that uncivilized mess, but the idea that somebody, anybody would say no, made him less afraid.

But Don wasn't looking for a woman. He was ready to rest for a while. Nothing about the life with a woman ever seemed to work out right. He wasn't looking, but Jonnie found him. "What you need, Mr. Don?" "You had all you want Mr. Don?" Every time he stepped foot in the tiny restaurant, until she finally dropped the *mister* altogether. Don knew what Jonnie was doing, feeling out her power, seeing if she could make an old man light up just because she wanted him to. Don understood all that. He decided that he didn't care.

Friday was fried-fish day, good croakers with crisp cornmeal overcoats on their itty-bitty bodies and black rubbery skin. Mae and Jonnie sold sandwiches every Friday, and the line ran out the door and into the yard. Men and women, but mostly men, crunching and spitting little bones all up and down the pitted road. Four Fridays before Devon's accident, Don was eating at Sisters like usual, standing in the yard when the Martin sisters, real sisters less than a year apart, started to sing two-part harmony, "His eye is on the sparrow, I know he watches me." Generations of Martins sing in churches, devil-music bands, and then back to churches, but how unusual for them to break into song just like that. Don loved the combination of their high rich voices, their almost identical faces, and their sweet bow-lipped mouths opening at the same time. He loved listening while he ate the hot-sauce-soaked white bread with the greasy fishy taste of the fresh catch. Jonnie told him later how she watched his face that day. How sad and unloved he seemed, she said. If Don's face looked sad, he couldn't help it. Don wanted to tell her that people take the insides of themselves, put it on someone else's face, but it wouldn't do any good to tell her that. There are things you learn from words and gestures, the sad human mistakes of others and there are things you can only get through the bitter taste on your own smooth tongue.

"What were you thinking?" she asked him later.

"Nothing," he said, which was true, but she believed that she and Don had shared their first secret moment, mistaking Don's silence and maybe even ignorance for a strong back.

Later that same day, Don took Jonnie to his home, a tiny rented trailer in the back of Sammie Wilson's yard. They were both shy. Don had been with girls since he was fourteen and women not long after that. He knew sex wasn't what you think. Women are all afraid they'll look bad, have people laughing and shaking their heads because they put themselves on the line, body and all, to believe in something. The idea that they might get ill-used made them crazy. Even a mild woman will break every dish in the house if she whiffs betrayal. Don had seen it. But Jonnie didn't want to know any better than to believe.

Jonnie sat cross-legged on Don's ancient couch. Don thought she looked like a spider with all those spindly arms and legs, in her tiny T-shirt, shorts creeping up her high tail. Don felt dirty looking at her slight body and tried to watch her mouth, concentrate on what she was saying. But Don couldn't shake that Jonnie looked like a child. He'd never hurt a child, a fact even his wife who mostly hated him wouldn't deny. Still, the creeping feeling that he had suddenly become the kind of nasty, broke-down heel leeching the life out of some young body was hard to take on.

"How old are you?" Don said with as much tenderness as he could, but he realized he sounded harsh.

Jonnie laughed, but she sensed that inside this innocuous question was a test she couldn't pass. "Old enough," trying to sound playful, but ending up sounding like a pouty child.

Don wasn't sure what he wanted to hear or what age would stop the magic, fix the image so they had to stop exactly where they were. There was nothing wrong with sitting with a young woman, even a beautiful one, even one he desired. Nothing in the world had happened that couldn't be backed down from, explained away as a moment of silly weakness.

"No, baby, how old?"

Jonnie hesitated, played at cleaning her fingernails. "Twenty-three if you need to know."

"Go on home."

Jonnie laughed, but she was scared. Don was a grown man with grown children, and she had the power to frighten him. Love is grown in poorer climates, even she knew that, but she wanted Don to be full up with her, consume his thinking, his desires, so much so that he couldn't remember to be wary and sad. She rolled the tiny T-shirt up and over her head, slowly, though she tried not to think about a striptease, tried to forget about her body nearly flat everywhere except for an inexplicable roll of fat below her bra. She stood up to wriggle out of her tiny shorts, tried not to notice that Don had modestly turned his head. Jonnie wanted to show Don that she was confident, not somebody's piss-ass child at all, but she wished she had hips to show him, big legs, and a full backside, a body that would make him sure about anything.

"Want to see my birthmark?" Jonnie turned her leg, her inner thigh pointed in Don's direction, to a dark amoeba-shaped mark the size of a silver dollar that looked like a splat of used chewing tobacco or spilled acid on her otherwise slick amber skin.

"Ugly, ain't it?" Don said.

Jonnie looked around for her shoes. Don laughed, but he wasn't sure what to do. He didn't mean to hurt her feelings. Young women often don't know when a thing is hurtful or just laughably true, nothing to be done about it.

"It is ugly, but you're not supposed to say that," Jonnie smiled, softening her reaction. She slid her feet into run-over sneakers and turned the corner to the kitchen.

Jonnie's behind eased out of her high-leg underwear as she walked. She pulled the elastic leg hole from one of her cheeks, like she and Don had known each other all their lives. "You want a drink?" she called, her head hanging out of the refrigerator.

"No, baby," he said. The common domestic gesture, Jonnie's eager face questioning, eased his tension some. "Yeah, bring me a co-cola."

She seemed to be staying.

But like most things, Jonnie didn't just change Don's life all at once. She didn't stay that night, but the next night after the restaurant closed she was there and the next, every day bringing clothes, a lamp,

278

shabby cotton curtains to replace the blue velvet dust catchers in the living room and other small items and knickknacks to mark the place as hers. Don was embarrassed that he didn't have any of the trappings of a real home, that all of his furniture in the trailer put together wasn't worth the effort to throw it out. Jonnie didn't seem to notice, or if she did, she didn't care a great deal. Don knew he was being stupid, but he thought worse of Jonnie for that acceptance, for being so young and not wanting more.

After a few days, she brought her little girl to visit, Sasha, a sweet little thing with curly hair the color of sand. Don had seen Sasha before at the restaurant, but she always stayed close to her grandmother and never let Mae get more than an arm's reach from her sight. If Jonnie came to stay for good, Don wasn't sure where Sasha would end up. You'd have to kill Mae to get that little girl away from her, and Don had no desire to fight. Jonnie might. You never knew what a mother would do to keep her child. Don didn't want to think about how Jonnie would react if it came to all that. If Don were being honest, he'd tell Jonnie that he didn't want the girl. His babies were all on the brink of adulthood, and it had been a long time since he'd had to talk to a little child, entertain them, or pretend to be interested in their tiny triumphs. Now he wasn't sure how much he could fake.

But that wasn't it. Don knew he shouldn't blame Sasha but couldn't quite get over that her daddy was a white man from the Love Valley Church Jonnie belonged to for a short time. The child couldn't help who her daddy was, Don knew that. She had no say at all over who brought her into the world. But every time he looked at her soft hazel eyes he felt something close to betrayal, a sickly uneasiness that went with anything associated with white people.

It didn't help that Jonnie met the man at an Eternal Masters in Search of Enlightenment meeting. That's what they called themselves. Don, of course, called them other things. A whole group of them lived together not in one house but by spells. Two of them, then three, then switch up. Every week they'd met in the leader's basement and talk and share food. Jonnie missed the talking with people who seemed to be interested about her life problems and her daily struggles to be good. Religion shouldn't smell musty, Don told her again and again about her basement church. But she missed it. Especially the dancing. Everyone in the flock was taught to waltz. Dancing is what brought Sasha's father into Jonnie's arms and his smooth-flowing rhythm, his careful way of finessing her into turns, his small, dainty little dips. The day he found out that Jonnie was pregnant, he waltzed out of that basement, out of the county, and by the time Jonnie heard tell of him, she couldn't really remember anything but the dancing that she liked about him. Turns out there's not that much enlightenment in the world. But even that love gone wrong wasn't enough to totally sour Jonnie on the Eternal Masters. She loved the idea of good country people, black and white, mostly white in their bare feet, spinning on someone's old shag carpet like members of the royal family.

Jonnie even taught Don to waltz. He didn't want to at first and briefly considered letting that be the first time that he told Jonnie no, but he finally decided to wait until he had something more important to protest. As it turned out, he liked it. He thought about loving it but wouldn't commit to loving a new thing, not at this late date, but he couldn't deny that the oompah-pah music, the swishing across the floor, holding a woman lightly but with precision like holding a tool, took him out of his head like nothing he'd done in a long time.

The day before Devon's accident, Don had to get up early to get Jonnie to the restaurant. Saturday was their biggest day, and Mae and Jonnie had hours of preparation work to do to get the lunches and dinners carryout ready.

"You coming by for dinner?"

"I'll be by to pick you up, but I'm not sure about dinner."

"Be here by seven, okay? I'll miss you."

Don gripped the steering wheel tighter, hoping Jonnie wouldn't notice. "I'll be here, baby."

Jonnie got out of the car, wiggle-walked for Don's benefit on the concrete path to the restaurant. She turned to watch him.

Don hadn't moved but watched Jonnie play her game. Framed by the picnic tables on one side, the thick yellow grass, and on both sides, low-reaching poplar branches' spring-green leaves highlighting Jonnie in the center, her chin just over her bare shoulder, her face expectant and bright.

"I'm a lucky man," Don yelled. But even as he said it, he realized that this was the first time he was telling Jonnie what he knew she wanted to hear.

Don waited on the back deck of Sylvia's house. She was a busy woman, what with the kids, her crazy family, her equally crazy friends with their constant low-rent problems, but Don knew she liked to be home on Saturdays. He wouldn't have to wait long. Don took a seat on the stairs leading up to the deck. Sylvia had her flower beds cleaned and neat, already prepared for summer growth. Sylvia might not keep a neat house, but her yard was another story altogether.

Sylvia had pots of various sizes on the deck and on the built-in bench above it. Little pots, terra-cotta, plastic ones, pots all over the place that she'd bought at garage sales and thrift stores, all full of seedlings bursting out of the red-clay soil she'd scraped up from the yard. This tacky mess grown on a few dimes would in the summer become Sylvia's lush garden with great masses of old-fashioned color in a jungle all over: bleeding heart, sweet peas, purple coneflower, even some showy annuals as long as she could grow them from seed. When they were very poor and not just ordinary poor, years ago, Sylvia would find birdseed and plant giant sunflowers around their trailer. Don loved their great brown faces, and though he never told her, thought Sylvia herself a magician for willing them into being. Don searched the pots for the

Magic Marker shorthand only Sylvia understood. He liked her simple printing, a man's
way of writing, bold and unadorned.

Last time he came, Sylvia wouldn't speak
to him at all. She peeled potatoes at the
sink. Water steaming hot as she stroked a
brush across the speckled potato bodies.
The water sang into the silver sink, making
Don content. Sylvia looked to have forgotten he was there and concentrated on the
sweet-looking potatoes, not soft or mealy
looking, but plump, just the size to fit nicely
in a fist. Don arranged the junk in his
pockets, gum, receipts, a cigarette stub he'd
fished out of Sylvia's garden.

"You gonna wash them all day," he said,
not particularly hateful, but he could tell
that he took Sylvia's moment and ruined it.
Before she had time to really think about it,
Sylvia threw the knife into Don's leg
propped on the chair in front of him.

"What the hell? Sylvia!" Don watched the
blood rush through his white sock onto his
fingers. It was a good shot, but not fatal,
anyone could see that. Still, Sylvia wanted
to feel something, rush to Don with genuine
concern. But all she could manage to do
was pull another knife out of the drawer
and continue washing the potatoes.

Sylvia rolled her car around the corner,

parked, hesitated just a minute trying to pretend she didn't see Don on the deck. She grabbed the canvas tote bag she was using for a purse and considered looking at herself in the rearview mirror to get some idea what Don was about to see. No reason, she thought. Might as well get it over with.

"What are you doing here?" Sylvia opened the car's back hatch, grabbed a grocery bag, motioned for Don to pick up the other one.

"Nothing. Just come to talk to you."

"Well, you better talk quick, I'm getting ready to go to sleep." Sylvia hoisted the bag to her hip, fiddled for her keys.

"You're not asleep now," Don said.

Don was always saying something stupid like that, Sylvia thought. Always trying to get her off her guard. If he said something dumb enough it was like a smack in the middle of the forehead, stunning you into silence, and he could keep on doing what he wanted. You don't spend twenty-four years messing around with a man and not learn at least a few of his tricks.

"Come on then. Put the meat in the freezer."

Don wriggled the damp packages of chicken breasts, short ribs, and hamburger from the plastic bag and stacked them in the corner behind the ice pops. He would have liked a little more to do, keep his hands busy and moving, let Sylvia see him working. She always liked him in motion, doing a chore, sweating, proving he had a plan. His luck, he was in the middle of a break when she decided to check on him, either leaning on a hoe, resting his eyes, or in a just-took-off-my-shoe-to-remove-a-stone position, the exhibit A to her belief that he was of little use and couldn't be trusted.

Don eased into the tweedy den chair and felt into the dark sides for a remote control.

Sylvia began folding the pile of towels in a mound at the end of the couch. She popped the cotton, smoothed each with the side of her hand. Don watched her pop and fold a few while the lint flew in the already stiff air around them. Don tried to latch onto one piece of lint and follow it to the ground, but the mote kept disappearing before his eyes.

"If you're just going to sit there, you could fold some. How long you staying anyway?" Sylvia threw a pile of towels to Don on the recliner. He tried to imitate Sylvia's actions, but he was slow.

"That's not very polite," Don said, pretending to be hurt. Sylvia laughed through her teeth, the sudden air sounding like a hiss in the room.

286

"I just come to see how you are, that's all."

"You see me every day, Don. You know how I am."

"I know."

"How's that little girl you've shacked up with?"

Don was surprised though he shouldn't have been. Of course Sylvia would find out about Jonnie. There are no secrets in a small town, Don had learned that the hard way.

"She's all right. All right. A little girl."

Sylvia laughed and rubbed the smooth skin on her neck, her nervous habit. Don watched her unmanicured hands rest on her thighs, form baskets of dark, thick fingers, protectors for her knees. Don kneeled in front of Sylvia, put his head on the fleshy part of her thigh. He didn't want Sylvia to see his face just then.

"You ever going to let me come back here?" Don said into the soiled denim of Sylvia's lap.

"Why should I? I see you more now than I ever did," Sylvia said, but what she wanted to say was underneath that meanness, a smooth thing like a river pebble, cool words that would make him come back and for good and finally be the man she could want.

Don raised his head and looked up into

Sylvia's face.

"You got a soda?"

"You can look."

Don grunted his way up, his skinny legs like pipe cleaners in his blue jeans. Sylvia wondered what he might have looked like if he'd fattened up a little. She'd figured he would, though she never pushed it. Most men don't stay rail thin, but spread in the middle, their faces broaden in a way she thought manly. Not Don. He was strong though, stronger than he looked. Sylvia thought his hair especially unruly today, spiky like the goldenrod bushes she liked, uncut, not careful shrubs, but radiant and irreverent. She knew that wildness was nothing to admire. Anything out of control was beautiful only to the distant looker, the woman passing by swiftly in the moving car.

Don drank the orange soda his kids favored. He hated the too-sweet syrup, but it was something. He didn't forget about Jonnie, a sweet girl. But anybody paying attention knew they weren't a forever couple. That was easy math. Sylvia would always be in the picture, it was as simple as that.

The kitchen was his favorite part of the house. Each instrument, pan, and object had a reason to be, a function you could name. There had been days when he let himself in the house just to look around and touch the hard things with purpose, the oversized spoons, turners, and graters, pots and chopping boards, all there, all seeming more necessary that he was.

Sylvia was still folding the raggedy towels, creasing the stained washcloths, stacking them for the closet. The fact that she hadn't moved made Don bold.

"That hit the spot," he sighed.

"Do you know anything you haven't heard before?" Sylvia rolled her eyes at Don's willing face.

"Come down here."

"I'm not getting on no floor with you."

"It's clean. Come on."

"I do the cleaning around here, and I know it ain't. Forget it. I need to take a nap anyway."

"Do you still love me, baby?" Don hadn't meant to say that. It wasn't a trick or some line to get Sylvia's attention, but an honest question, one he wanted to know the answer to.

"Why do you want to start all that mess?" Sylvia yelled, flecks of angry spit that landed on Don's cheek. The meanness of it startled him, almost made him cry.

"I don't know," he said as he reached up to her, coaxed her shoulders forward, guided her to the floor. She rested her head on his shoulder, though that's not what she was set on doing at all. She looked twisted and uncomfortable leaning into him like that, and Don worried over the contortions Sylvia had to do to be close. Don smoothed her hair, wanting Sylvia to be soothed, if just for a minute, like she was finally okay, finally awake from a bad dream. He loved the way Sylvia could open herself up for him, as easily and quickly as a child, her ire and disappointment forgiven or at least held in abeyance as her body slackened and fear rippled through and then escaped her face like an ousted demon.

"Did you comb your hair today?" he said.

"Did you?" she whispered.

The bed was heaped with clothes, clean and dirty, some free weights Sylvia always planned to use with her exercise tape, and her large rolling suitcase.

"You going somewhere?" Don asked, a flutter of nerves wiggling its way into his stomach.

"Where am I gonna go?" Sylvia snapped. "Lana wanted it."

Don ignored her tone, tried not to let Sylvia see his exhale of relief. "Lana's always wanting something."

"Don, let her alone, she don't need to be in this."

Don took off his shirt, then his jeans. "She ain't welcome as far as I'm concerned."

Sylvia stood in front of the bed waiting for directions. Nothing about Sylvia was shy, but her relationship with Don, this marriage that wasn't a marriage confused her, took her to uncharted land where she didn't understand the customs.

"You want to dance?" he whispered.

Sylvia grinned. She looked so young when she grinned, and Don felt a surge of warmth for her, for the fun young girl who drank beer as well as he ever did, let the foam dribble on her chin, if she wanted. The girl who from the day he saw her naked liked for him to take in her whole long body, her legs thick and strong as tree trunks, the pooch of her belly, her big heavy breasts, nipples dark as plums. She convinced him that she was the way a woman should look, and anything else was a compromise. At first he was afraid to tell her how good she was and lived in terror that she would realize the whole truth and walk away. A young man won't believe that holding back the truth won't keep a woman close.

Sylvia's face was glad, unmired by worry, the only time she was truly a beautiful woman. Her grandmother's freckles weren't pinched into a seagull shape on her cheeks, her mother's disappointed mouth was finally twisted into happiness.

"Here, look at my face, but follow my feet," Don pulled her into his body.

In his embrace, Sylvia knew Don was following a script he'd learned from another woman. Sylvia knew that men need direction from the woman they choose. It makes them feel cared for and safe. She leaned into Don's naked chest and tried to pretend that was all there was to it. She was the most stable part of Don's world. Always had been. He would stray, but didn't he always come back? Didn't he end up wanting her? But feeling his body move from the care he'd taken from that child hurt her more than she'd anticipated. Sylvia remembered when Jonnie was born, a fat, bald-headed baby with the mystery father. Sylvia had held her not as a baby, but when she was a bigger child, a toddler, Sylvia was sure she'd hefted that girl in the crook of her own arm.

Don's leg caressed her thigh and shifted her weight to the other foot, moved her, however awkwardly into a tiny square in the space between her disheveled bed and the wall. She wasn't going to cry, although she thought about it. But as quickly as it came, she felt the old hardness build, the dike that kept Don away from the best part of herself.

Don realized he'd made a mistake though he wasn't quite sure what it was. He felt the stiffness return to Sylvia, the closed-off place he hated in her that would one day brick up against him.

"Come on baby," he said. "We don't have to mess around with that. I just want to be here with you."

Sylvia swiped the clothes from the bed, leaned to the footboard, and untangled the complicated sheets. She should divorce this man. The same reasons she told him again and again to leave and don't come back were the reasons she should make it legal, go ahead and sign the papers. But not today. No one had noticed her today. Not the girl at the Bi-Lo supermarket, who didn't pause as she looked around her to the next customer, not the teenage boys, all baseball caps and oversized shirts loud-talking outside of Lana's hair salon, not the old man at the gas station on the other side of the pump, watching the numbers roll on the display like he was hoping against all hope that seven would not follow six, just this once, and none of the passing people in the mountain town, not another soul, besides this man, had thought to remember that Sylvia Ross was even alive.

"Are you staying, Don?"

Don reached his fingers to the clasp of her bra, popped it open like a combination lock. "How long you need me, baby?"

ACKNOWLEDGMENTS

Some of the stories in this collection were previously published, some in slightly different form, in the following journals and anthologies: "Family Museum of the Ancient Postcards" in *New Letters* and *New Stories from the South,* 2009; "If You Hit Randolph County, You've Gone Too Far" in *Tampa Review;* "We Are Taking Only What We Need" in *Oxford American;* "Unassigned Territory" in *Oxford American, New Stories from the South,* 2007, and *Pushcart XXXII: Best of the Small Presses,* 2008 edition; "Highway 18" in *Tartts Four: Incisive Fiction from Emerging Writers;* "Welcome to the City of Dreams" (as "Talk to Me While I'm Listening") in *New Writing: The International Journal for the Practice and Theory of Creative Writing.*

I owe great debts of gratitude to many but especially to Rod Santos and Lynne Mc-

Mahon, mentors in writing and life. Many thanks go to the Creative Writing Program at the University of Missouri-Columbia and Marly Swick and Trudy Lewis. My professors at the University of North Carolina at Charlotte, Sandra Govan, Stan Patten, and Nanci Kincaid, gave me hope and inspiration when I needed it most. Marc Smirnoff and Carol Ann Fitzgerald at the *Oxford American* offered their invaluable support and careful attention to my work. I am so grateful. I cannot thank Jan Fergus enough for her vision, insight, and love. I am blessed to count her as my friend.

Great thanks to my dear ones: my baby brothers, Joel, Marc, Brent, and Mitchell, and to my sisters, Keya and Kellie.

To the Watts family: Gary, Luke, Jim and Charlie, but especially to the good-looking, good-cooking women: Mary Watts, beloved Grammy; Mary S., Savannah, Molly and the cool aunts Bernadette, Terry, and Gale. I am proud to call you family.

Many thanks to my friends who provided support and inspiration: Tina Wilson, Betsy Fifer, Joanie Mackowski, Seth Moglen, Beth Dolan, and Monica Najar. And to the beautiful amazing women who have made the good times great and bad times bearable: Kristin Handler, Vera Fennell, Julia

Maserjian, Holona Ochs, and Angela Scott.

To Alex Doty, I still can't believe you are gone. Thank you. You made this book and my life richer.

To my parents, Brenda Wray and Billy Powell. I told you I had a book in me, Daddy.

To my dear grandmother Ruby P. Dula: I will never stop missing you.

ABOUT THE AUTHOR

Stephanie Powell Watts won the Ernest J. Gaines Award for Literary Excellence for her debut story collection, *We Are Taking Only What We Need (2012), also named one of 2013's Best Summer Reads by O: The Oprah Magazine. Her short fiction has been included in two volumes of the Best New Stories from the South anthology and honored with a Pushcart Prize.*
Born in the foothills of North Carolina, with a PhD from the University of Missouri and a BA from the University of North Carolina at Charlotte, she now lives with her husband and son in Pennsylvania where she is an associate professor at Lehigh University.

Her website can be found at: http://stephaniepowellwatts.com/